The Dream Stone

The Dream Stone

A novel

Bountiful Blessings!

Regina Daly

Regina Daly

The Dream Stone is a work of fiction, and the events, incidents, locations, and characters are the product of the author's imagination or are used fictitiously. Any resemblance to events, actual locations, or persons, living or dead, is entirely coincidental.

Book cover design by Anne Giordano

ISBN 978-1-7964-4478-0

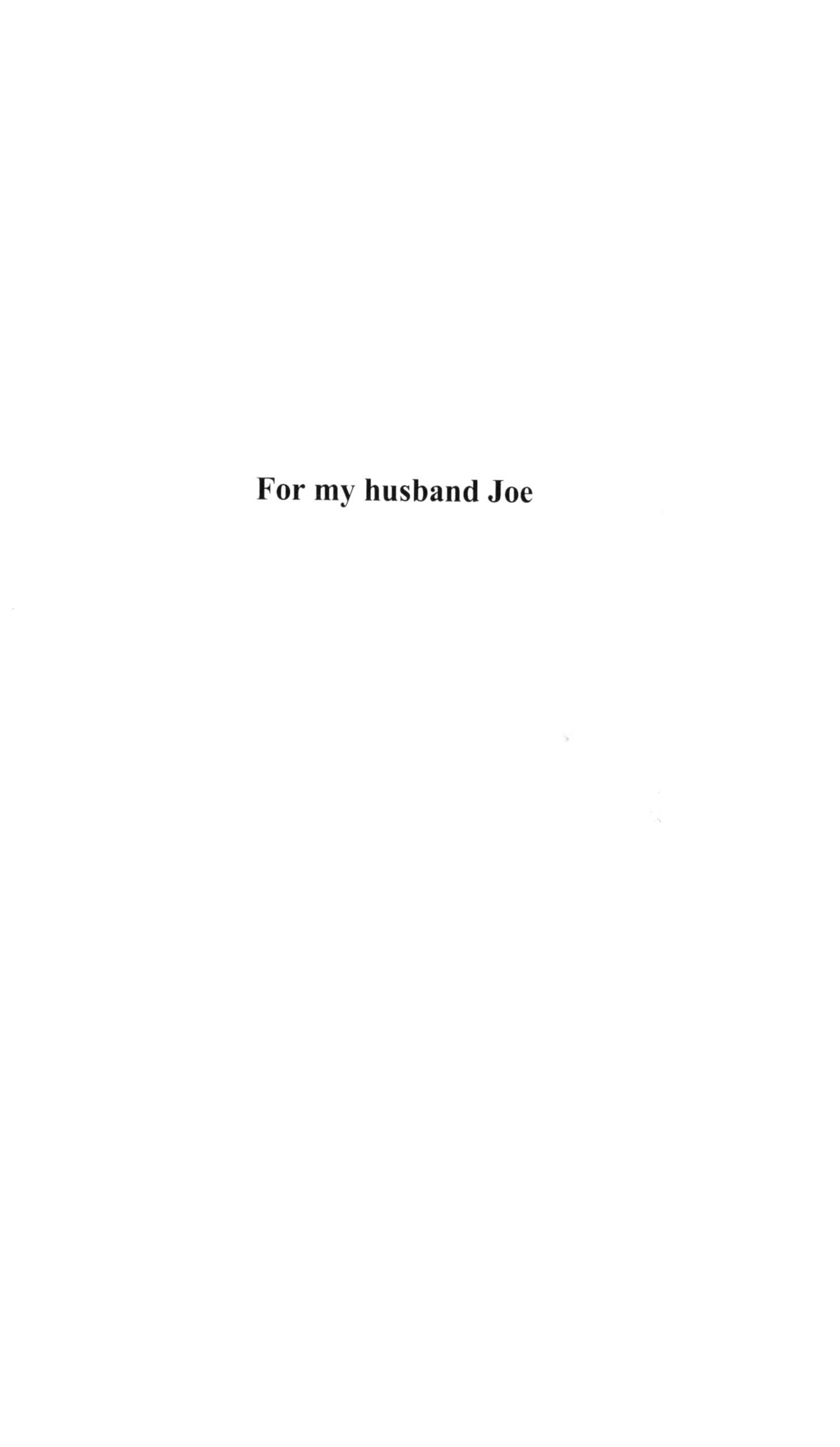

For my husband Joe

Contents

PART ONE

Annie 11
Charlene 18
Childhood Struggles 26
Travel Plans 34
Fishing Buddies 42
A Challenging Dream 51
The Prayer Meeting 61
Dinner with the Rhineharts 67
Micah's Confession 72
Rebecca and Tim's Story 83
An Eye-Opening Trip 86
Sisterly Advice 95
Annie's Confession 102
The Announcement 107
News from Far Away 115

PART TWO

Arrival in Colombia 131
Breaking Through Pain 142

Micah's Dream 150
Drilling 158
Stateside 166
Susan and Emma 176
The Question 181
Epilogue 186
Acknowledgments 191

PART ONE

* * * *

Annie

An image of an egret wearing a diamond anklet was etched into the pink glass door of the exquisitely-designed jewelry shop. The dazzling gems perched inches above the bird's foot caught the sunlight as a delightful chime whispered the arrival of the young woman.

The owner looked up to see the petite blonde whose turquoise blouse mirrored her crystal eyes. She wore a hint of a fresh fragrance by Clinique and not enough jewelry. He assessed: stylish but a tad understated. I have the perfect piece that would grace her neck superbly. The man stepped out from behind the display case to greet the young woman as he imagined the unique 'Argentinian tear drop' resting elegantly on her delicate neck. It was an older piece, but he was certain she could showcase the gem as it deserved.

"How may I help you today?"

Annie smiled demurely, "Could you take a look at this stone and appraise it?"

He hesitated. Then his eyes fell upon the stone cradled in a royal blue cloth which Annie held in her slightly extended hand. His face remained stolid. After a brief pause, he adjusted the headlamp back onto his head and reached for the stone. First, he balanced it by giving it a feather light bounce in an open palm as if he could calculate its exact weight. He continued to shine his lamp on the stone and asked, "Do you mind if I brush it with this soft cloth?"

"Not at all."

Turning the stone slowly in his hand, he began to walk towards the back room. He glanced over his shoulder at her. On cue, Annie straightened her back and followed him. The jeweler's voice had a familiar quiver when he asked, "How did you come to possess this stone?" She remembered playing poker with her brother Scott when they were kids. His quivery voice always signaled when he had a valuable hand.

Her eyes glinted with the reply, "I'd rather not say, for now."

He cocked his head slightly while squinting at her between magnifiers and the head lamp. She gave a dismissive shrug of her right shoulder. He turned and lowered himself into the brown leather chair and quickly scrolled to a site specifically for jewelers. After a few minutes of investigating, he faced Annie and recited a long disclaimer about not being held liable for quoting any specific monetary value. She flicked the edge of the man's business card and continued to unconsciously crease it back and forth.

She knew the man was talking, but her mind wandered and only heard the conclusion, "Miss, I would be glad to give you an excellent price for a thorough evaluation of the stone or offer you a fair market price to purchase it."

When she reached for the stone, the jeweler did not give it up too easily. He repeated, "I'd give you a good price."

She looked at him and could picture Scott smirking. She shook her head, "Thanks for your time. I'd like to stop by next week to check out some of the beautiful charm bracelets in your showcase."

He reluctantly released the stone into the velvet cloth. Walking out the door, her wiry thoughts replayed the events of two days ago when the gem first caught her eye. It was not exactly on the bike path when it glistened in the sunshine.

Kneeling and reaching under some of the pickets of the old wooden fence gave her access to the unusual green rock. She shook her head, remembering how she had to scrub the grass stains from the knees of her cute blue capris when she got home that afternoon.

Now her mind was listing all the reasons this stone was legitimately hers. Obviously from the reaction of the jeweler, the irregular green rock was worth something. The owners of the old home did not know it was there. They probably never even walked back to that part of their slightly overgrown yard. A rainstorm could have easily pushed it into the yard. No, the stone was definitely hers! No doubt about it, she was the owner and began rehearsing the phrase, "Possession is nine tenths of the law."

* * * *

Annie continued her quest the next day by casually riding her bike in front of the house. The elderly lady was watering a lovely flower garden with one of those expandable hoses. There was a pretty array of pink vincas and tufts of lavender arranged neatly on the sun-drenched side of the house. Annie was envisioning sitting with her and asking if she wanted to sell her home. That would guarantee she would be the rightful owner of the stone. Each rehearsed conversation sounded hollow at best. Her mind was battling with some crazy scenarios. As she pedaled slowly past the house, the owner looked up and waved pleasantly.

Am I crazy? Am I really trying to find ways to justify keeping this stone? What has gotten into me? The jeweler never even quoted a price. His reaction was such a Scott move. Which leads me to believe it might be valuable. My husband and I are quite comfortable; we certainly don't need any financial help. What ***IS*** *the hold this stupid stone has over me?*

Wallowing in disappointment and disgruntled by the fact the jeweler would not even give her a general idea of the value, she did not notice the ball rolling fast in her direction. It bounced against her front wheel and sent Annie tumbling. There was a frightened young voice shouting apologies as she took a nosedive to the ground. Landing hard on her right forearm, she felt the handlebar angrily poke into her ribs. The wheel continued to spin dangerously close to her face. The boy struggled to lift the bike and when the garden hose lady helped him, Annie could finally sit up. Gentle hands brushed some grass off her hair. Grandma and the boy helped to steady and guide the dazed cyclist to their front porch.

The lady disappeared into the house as she instructed, “Micah, you wait here, Lita will be right back.”

The child squatted near Annie and just kept looking at her face and arm. "Oh boy, lucky your angels were wif you or you’d be ridin’ in the am-be-lance."

Surely, she didn't hear him correctly. Was he really talking about angels? Returning to the porch, his grandmother began wiping off the bloody arm and applying some ointment and a bandage.

"Are you a nurse?” Annie squeaked out, realizing how upset she was. She couldn’t recall the last time she fell off her bicycle.

“No, dear, not by profession.”

Annie wondered if she hit her head too. Usually she would only be annoyed at this whole situation but instead she felt strangely comforted and cared for by these two. The whole scene felt surreal.

The five-year-old was holding the offending ball near Annie, "Sorry my favorite ball tripped ya. Here, it’s for you. It bounces real good."

“Oh no, I don't want it,” she told the kid. A souvenir of this fall was not her idea of a good memory.

"When your arm gets better, ya can have fun wif it. It makes me smile. Maybe it can help *you* smile, too."

She scrunched her nose at him and thought, *I'm a smiley person. You don't know me. Nobody who takes a header off their bike feels like smilin', so back off kid!*

The lady said, "I'm Emma and this is my grandson Micah. Let me get us some cookies and home-brewed iced tea."

Annie was too stunned to decline the offer. She thought, *they probably want to avoid a lawsuit.* But there was something genuine about their caring for her. She decided to relax and enjoy the attention. Besides, maybe she could gather some valuable information about the stone.

Micah seemed happy that the stranger finally agreed to keep the ball. It was his way of extending an apology. He sat quietly watching her. He was quick to avoid eye contact when Annie looked up at him. She asked him, "How long have you lived here?" Micah looked down and began humming and picking at some unseen speck on his jeans.

Emma approached with a beautiful wooden tray laden with delicate teacups, a pitcher of iced tea, and some delicious-smelling cookies. The tray was stunning with uniquely carved handles and inlaid wood.

Micah stood close to Emma as he held his face to her apron, "Can I go swing now?"

She squeezed him and said, "Sure, sweetheart. Remember, it was just an accident."

Micah looked sorrowfully at his grandmother, "Accidents are stupid." He made a bee-line sprint to the side of the house.

Annie turned to her, "Excuse me, did you tell me your name was Emma or Lisa?"

She looked at Annie quizzically, then smiled as she said, "Micah calls me Lita, he has called me that ever since he could talk."

"How precious," she responded half-heartedly. As soon as she uttered the word precious, it was as if her mind snapped to attention. She tried not to sound like a detective when she asked Emma a few questions about their living here. Emma offered only one or two answers and said, "Enough of us, let's get you home and schedule a proper visit real soon. You need some rest after that spill. My husband will give you a ride home in his truck and he'll put your bike in the back."

"That's not necessary," the younger woman replied.

"Apparently it is. He already looked at your bike, and he'll need a couple days to get a new tire."

When Annie turned around, the lady's husband was walking up to the porch wiping his hands on an old rag, "My name is Jackson Rhinehart, but most people call me Pops. I'd shake your hand, but I don't want to add oil to your bruised arm." His statement caused the girls to re-examine the injury.

Annie looked back at Jackson, "It coulda been worse."

"Looks like your bike needs more recovery time than you do. You ready to go home, young lady? I'll give you a lift."

"Sure, thanks."

Jackson said, "Well it's the least we can do since our grandson's ball took you out."

Emma smiled and said, "After your bike gets fixed, you can stop by for a visit. It was nice to meet you, Annie Livingston."

* * * *

Safely in her own room, Annie was soaking in her tub, pampering her sore body. Fortunately, the only signs of colliding into the bouncy ball were a few aches, and a black and blue arm. She dried off and slipped into sweats and her fuzzy pink slippers. Luke returned home from work and came into their bedroom to greet his wife. He stopped half way across the room when he saw Annie, "What happened to you?"

Holding up her arm, "This little thing. You should see the other guy." Luke's frown was riddled with question marks.

She quickly added, "Just kiddin'. My bike and I had a run-in with a little boy's very bouncy ball. Kids are cute, but they sure can be a nuisance. I'm glad we decided not to have any!"

"Where did all this happen?" Luke asked.

Annie filled him in on all the details of the accident. Well, not all the details. She knew Luke would think her behavior was rather odd. She wondered about her own peculiar behavior. She gave the highlights of the story and finished with, "My bike's in our garage with one tire until Emma's husband can fix it."

"Sounds like quite an eventful day. Want some tea or maybe something stronger?" Luke asked.

"Nah. But can we order Chinese? I don't feel like attempting to cook tonight."

"Sure, I'll go order. Do ya want anything special?"

"Yep, can I have a number ten and two egg rolls, please?"

When the food arrived, Luke spent a couple minutes dishing it out. It was hard for Annie to do her routine of balancing chopsticks with an injured arm. He leaned over and perched the sticks, so they rested in her hands. He said, "Okay, all is right with the world, we can eat Chinese food with balanced sticks." They looked at each other and laughed.

Annie was glad it was time to eat and that Luke was more concerned about her arm than the story she was hiding from him.

Charlene

The next morning, Annie was holding her coffee and staring out the back door when Luke came into the kitchen. Her hands were wrapped around the colorful cup she purchased on their trip to Costa Rica two years ago. The cup held fond memories of lush forests and refreshing waterfalls. Today it provided warmth and comfort as she pieced together last night's troubling dream.

He coughed, "Ahem."

She was startled. "I didn't hear you come in," she said, putting her mug on the counter.

"I noticed. You're up a little early, aren't you? Is your arm bothering you, Hon?"

"No, but a dream got me up. Funny how you only remember certain dreams. Anyhow, good morning, are you ready for coffee?"

"No, now I'm ready for a morning kiss," he said as he folded Annie into his arms. She rested snugly against his chest dropping her arm just under his reach. "Oh sorry," he stepped back. "Did I hurt you?"

"No, I'm okay." After they snuggled and kissed, they both sipped their coffees.

"Looks like it's already turning a stylish shade of black and blue. How's it feeling?"

"My arm feels throbby but my whole body feels beat up."

"Looks like a day off for you, sweetheart."

"I was already scheduled to have off today. I'll soak this arm and then I'm gonna call Charlie."

"You calling your sister about your fall or the dream?"

"Both, I guess. Time to use the skills she learned at the class. She's gonna like having a dream to interpret."

"So, do I get to hear this dream of yours? Or is it a secret?"

"No secret. It's rather mundane but let's give Charlene first crack at it." Annie giggled, "This is the first time I'm **really** curious as to what she might come up with."

Luke shot a quick look at the clock and put his coffee on the table. "I have to get going. I'll check on you later. Rest that arm." He leaned over and planted a light kiss on her cheek.

* * * *

After the third ring, Charlene answered the phone. "What's up, Sis?"

"Hey Charlie, how's it goin'? Thought you might like to hear a dream I had last night."

Charlene responded, "Oooh great, let me turn off the stove and grab a notepad."

She made her way over to the stove and balanced on her cooperative leg. She scooped up the pen that was lying in the new glass dish on the kitchen counter.

Annie listened to her sister shuffle about in the kitchen. Charlie said, "I have a pen. So, shoot."

"The dream's kinda short. But here goes. I was riding my bike and I fell asleep but didn't fall off the bike! It was like I was gliding on it. Then a flying 'being' began shaking my shoulder to wake me up. I was still on the bike when I woke up. End of dream."

Charlie asked, "Was it in color?"

"Yes, I can remember what I was wearing and how I felt."

"Good, go ahead and fill in any details."

"I was wearing jeans and sneaks and a green sweater. The bike was not really mine. It wasn't stolen or anything. The dream bike was blue, my real bike is black and red. When I woke up in bed, I felt very sleepy, like I needed more rest. Does that make ANY sense?"

"Well, like with any dream, I'll pray first and see if I get any interpretation. Sometimes I don't have a clue what they mean, at least for a few days. I'll let you know when I do get something. Be patient, little sister, Okay?"

"Yeah, yeah, I'll keep busy and not hold my breath."

"What cha doin' today, Annie?"

"I need to recover. My bike and I had a little run-in with a kid's ball yesterday. By the look of my bruised arm, I think the ball won."

Charlie gasped and said, "Oh my gosh, are you okay?"

"Yeah, Sis, it was just a little mishap."

Charlene told Annie, "I **do** think if you tell me about your accident, it might have something to do with your dream." She added, "I'm getting ready to work in my garden today, the side bed needs attention. Wanna come over and keep me company? You can tell me about your fall."

"Sure, sounds better than sitting around here solo all day."

"Can you drive your car?"

"Yes, I can drive. I'll take you up on your offer. If you have any of those brownies left, can I get one?"

"Those are long gone."

Annie rolled her eyes and mumbled to herself quietly, "Kids, hmph." Into the phone, she said, "No worries. I'll see you in an hour... ish."

* * * *

Annie was glad her sister only lived ten minutes away. Charlie said, "Ouch," when she saw the bandaged arm. She added, "You shoulda worn your black and blue sweater to match that!"

The younger sister replied, "My ego was bruised more than my arm. And hey, no cutting on the injured party here." The girls hugged, and Charlene said the rocking chairs were waiting for them.

Annie cocked her head toward her sibling and asked, "You feeling okay? I thought you said you were gonna weed the side garden."

"Nah, sitting with my kid sister sounds better for today."

Annie looked to her hostess trying to read her body language. *Is she hurting today? Seems like I'm feeling sorry for myself and this sister of mine might be the one who's hurting.* Charlene had a quiet, confident sparkle in her eyes and it put Annie at ease. They could spend some uninterrupted time together, at least before the kids starting streaming in the door.

Charlene reached into the freezer and pulled out a Ziploc bag. Dangling it in the air she waved it at her sister. Annie gave a sly look and asked, "Is that what I think it is?"

"Here, just for you. I always try to stash one or two away for someone who might need a special treat. Looks like you're it today."

Annie reached for the brownies and went over to pour two cups of coffee. "You never stop looking out for me, huh?" She thought how much she admired her older sister.

When you visit Charlene, you feel like you take a step back in time. Some of her children's artwork is displayed in ornate frames. Those masterpieces range from the scribblings of a three-year-old to the more mature artist strokes of a teenager. Her Christmas tree with simple white lights sits in the corner of her front porch year-round. The ornaments are symbols of some of the things the kids have accomplished over the years. Annie's favorite one is Liz's writing pen with the white quill. A sweet memory of when her niece had one of her writings published in a literary magazine. There also hangs a tiny pair of running shoes, representing Mark's participation in the local 'Run for Cancer'. Andrew's soccer ball adorns the lower limb because it is right where a seven-year-old can reach it. There are lots of cherished memories hanging from those limbs.

The décor throughout their home is simple and says, "Home Sweet Home." Charlene is an amazing baker and loves to work in the garden.

She is slow and methodical in every task she does because the MS dictates her pace.

When Charlene was diagnosed with Multiple Sclerosis five years ago, it sounded like a death sentence to everyone in the family. Although it was primarily Charlene and Ray's burden to bear, Annie could never quite understand how such a difficult affliction could happen to a person as sweet and kind as her big sister. The diagnosis clung to Annie like a dark shadow. The thought of losing Charlene to MS after they had suffered so much loss during their own childhood made Annie shudder. That dreaded disease instilled a horrid fear that prevented her from ever imagining having kids of her own. How could she take a chance of having children? What if she got Multiple Sclerosis, too? What if she died and left the kids orphaned? It was unbearable for her to think of the possibility of afflicting children, if she ever had them.

"Annie, do you feel all right?"

"Yeah, I'm okay. I'll cream the coffees and meet you at the rocking chairs. I'll give you a head start."

"Teasing me? It finally sounds like you're lightening up. That's a good thing, Sis." Annie set the mugs next to each chair and resumed her musings as they enjoyed rocking quietly.

MS gets handled like other challenges Charlene has had in life. She drew near to the Lord rather than withdraw from Him when she got the diagnosis. Early in life Charlene learned to treat difficulties like a puzzle. She'd pick the easy pieces and set them in place and work with the harder pieces until they snapped into position. Annie thought of how her own life felt stuck, like the pieces just wouldn't fit into their place lately. Since her sister was such a good example of how to handle struggles, the younger sibling began to review how the elder dealt with some of those hurdles.

Annie remembered when the early stages of MS depleted Charlene's upper body strength quickly. She needed help walking and her arms couldn't grasp the crutches to give her enough support. At that time, their niece Suzanne was studying physical therapy. She talked about some newly developed, aerodynamic crutches that had been designed to be more user friendly than the standard ones. When Ray learned about the new and improved walking sticks, he gave Suzanne the go ahead to check out how much they cost. The girls' brother Scott and his wife stepped in and bought a pair of those amazing tools that have helped Charlie's walk to resemble a glide.

There have been lots of times over the past five years when friends and family have stepped in to assist Charlene and her husband Ray in dealing with all kinds of issues related to MS. Even though the struggles are monumental, she chooses to see the good in each situation. She loves to make lemonade out of mounds of lemons and has an incredible knack for making it look easy most of the time.

Her children inherited her sweet disposition. Her oldest son Mark is very organized and has used his administrative skill to put together a unique event for his mom. What started out as a relatively small gathering at the local V.F.W. has grown into an annual event and is now held in a banquet hall in a nearby town. It's a fundraiser to offset some of the 'extras' that are needed for his mom's care. Charlene shared that money with some local members in the MS support group who also needed a financial boost.

Mark's younger sister Liz had recently been caught up in the idea that her brother initiated. The local paper printed one of Liz's articles about the fundraiser. It generated interest in the MS event and added new supporters. Mark and Liz found creative ways to use their talents to help their mom and her buddies.

Annie knew the soft spot in her own heart for Andrew, the youngest member of Ray and Charlene's family. He is always on the go.

Fishing, hiking, biking, boarding, and lots of other activities. He's determined to squeeze every drop out of life. He has watched his mom and dad become less active recently, so he's living life for all three of them! He makes Charlene laugh. At the tender age of seven, he can create a whirlwind of energy. As much as Annie loves her nieces and nephews, she was glad to leave the heavy-duty responsibility of raising kids to her sister. There's too much worry required for that task. Annie snapped quickly out of her reveries when Andrew hopped off the yellow bus and ran towards his mom and aunt yelling, "Aunt Annie, did you bring any pretzels for me?" Charlie's dimples deepened and her eyes sparkled. Ever since Annie introduced him to the delicious treats from Auntie Anne's Pretzel store, he would ask for those yummy snacks. He thought she had a constant supply.

Since Andrew's arrival the girls knew he would command their attention. They asked about his day. He rattled off the two or three main events which involved the bus trip to school and playground activities. After the update, he jumped up, almost as if he just remembered to hug his mom and aunt. Annie noticed that he almost tackled her with his hug but with Charlene, his approach was tender as he squeezed his youthful energy into her. No wonder he holds a unique place in her heart.

While Andrew ran into the house, the girls could begin their conversation. Now it was time for Charlie to pepper her kid sister with questions about her fall and the lovely family that mended her wounds. Of course, Annie's story discreetly omitted the part about finding the stone.

After their visit, Annie got into the car to leave, Charlie assured her this line of questioning was not over. They laughed lightly, and she looked up and blew a kiss to Andrew as he hung his head out the window to yell, "Good-bye Aunt Annie, bring me a pretzel next time you come over, okay?"

On her way home, she took a slight detour to pass the house where she had fallen. She wanted to find out more about that family. Jackson had his head under the hood of his car and Micah was twirling on the rope swing. There was no sign of Emma.

It was time for Annie to go home.

Childhood Struggles

Back home sitting at the computer, Annie busied herself looking up any information she could find about the stone. The ice pack on her arm was slightly hindering her computer skills. She mused, *I'm glad I heard the jeweler mumble "Colombian Jade" under his breath. At least I have an idea of what to research.* An unpleasant smell caught her attention and she jumped up from her desk, dropping the ice pack to the floor. Sprinting to the kitchen she scolded herself, "Girl, either cook OR research. Don't do both at the same time. It does not work!"

* * * *

Just as Annie was pulling the meatloaf out of the oven, Luke walked in the door. "Mmm, huele bien (smells good)," he said in Spanish.

"Sí, señor, bienvenido a casa," (welcome home) she responded. She placed the hot casserole dish on the counter and in a single motion he dropped the mail on the desk and gave her a loving squeeze.

Annie thought, *my favorite place in the whole world is to be in this man's arms. When we hug, it melts any troubles away. Even though we don't mention dinner, I think we're both hoping this good-smelling meal will taste okay. We both know my expertise is not cooking. One of these days, I vow to myself, I will learn this mysterious art. If Julia Child could do it, so can I.* She stepped back from Luke and finished setting their dinner on the table.

Annie pushed the meat around on her plate while her mind got busy, *I wonder how Charlene got all the talent for cooking and baking? Uggh. My husband eats the appropriate amount of dinner before he takes his plate to the sink. Most of it is going in the garbage disposal because once again this meal gets added to the inedible list. Does he leave here and visit a fast food place to keep up his strength? Personally, I'm grateful for those ready-made packets of veggies, fruit, and cheese to keep myself going.*

After they relocated to the den, he looked at her arm and decided it was healing nicely.

Annie interjected casually, "Did I mention I found an unusual stone the other day on my bike ride?"

Luke raised his eyebrows, "No. Was that the same day you fell off the bike?"

"I did not just **fall** off my bike, I was catapulted off by a bouncy ball, remember?"

"Oh yeah, I forgot a little kid slammed you with his toy."

"Really, Luke, you can be a jerk sometimes. I woulda never taken that dive without some help."

"Okay, okay. So, tell me about this stone."

She filled Luke in on the parts of the story that gave her the most credibility. Even while she was telling her version, she felt uneasy. She was not in the habit of keeping anything from her husband. She couldn't pinpoint why so many uncertainties kept creeping up on her lately. When she told him the story, she included the part about the trip she took to the jeweler. At least she would try to come clean now. She concluded, "Luke, isn't it strange how it caught my eye from the bike path?"

He ignored the question, "This seems so out of character for you. Is something going on in your head that I don't know about?"

"I'm not even sure myself. It's weird. I kinda feel like a little kid searching for an adventure like the mystery adventurer Nancy Drew. You know the one my aunt used to talk about."

Luke's voice spiked, "Mystery character? Wait, now you think you're some mystery solver. Seriously, Annie, what's happening here?"

"No. I'm not sure how far I'm willing to go to check out this green gem, but I wanna check it out just a little more. It's not like I'm trying to find a hidden treasure or somethin'. There does seem to be a mystery to solve here. If a real treasure comes out of this whole adventure, then so be it." She did not intend for her response to sound so toxic.

He shot her a sulky frown.

* * * *

Three days after the accident, Annie was getting ready for work when the phone chirped the Brahms' Lullaby. That was Charlene's ring. She put her hot curling iron down and quickly checked the message to make sure there were no emergencies. Nope, no numbers with their special codes. She'll get back to her sister at lunch time.

Annie knew Charlene began the day very early because of all her personal challenges. She focuses her morning energy on getting the kids out the door to school. The whole family works together like a well-oiled machine.

Annie couldn't help but let her mind recall their own jumbled childhood. She loved Charlene, who for quite some time, was her mom, too!

Their mother had dealt with bouts of depression. Aunt Helen told us kids that mother tried to maintain her own fragile health while caring for us. The tasks exhausted her beyond repair. She disappeared when Annie was only thirteen months old.

Charlene became the little mommy for her younger brother and baby sister.

During the time when mother was still home with them, their dad learned to be both parents. Mom slept often, and she created such tension when she was awake. The two older children occupied themselves away from their mother. Charlene learned to diaper and feed baby Annie, who had become her own real live doll.

When mother left, it hardly altered the roles each family member had already assumed. Annie was too little to remember and Scott was a busy three-year-old. Only Charlene, at the tender age of five had any idea of the brokenness in their family. Charlene remembered hearing dad speak with Aunt Helen and mention something about a faraway place where people like mother could 'maintain'. Charlene thought that word meant a safe place for someone who was sick. Deep in her young heart she believed mommy would be back when she was all better.

Dad did his best to hold the family together, he was like a knight in shining armor to Annie. She adored her dad and respected Charlene like a mother. They did not have the luxury of bonding as sisters because of the family dynamic.

When Annie had school events, Dad was her biggest fan. In the first-grade play Annie had the role of the tree in the garden where the princess sat. Dad clapped so hard during the performance, the guy sitting next to him had asked, "Is the little princess yours?" Dad said, "Yep, the sweet little one wearing all the leaves. That's my princess!"

Dad's lap was never far when little Annie needed to snuggle. She spent hours telling him her dreams and all her little girl wishes. Occasionally, he even donned the required apron to sit with the dolls and his princess for tea time. Charlene and Scott each had their special times with their father, but Annie was the apple of his eye.

Roles were drastically changed when Annie was nearing the age of eight. Charlene was setting the table for dinner and Scott was pouring iced tea when the doorbell rang. Annie ran to the door as Charlene was yelling, "Don't open it. Wait till daddy gets home." But little Annie swung the door wide open to see two uniformed policemen standing on their front steps. The sequence of events after that encounter was a blur. At some point in the confusion of the evening, their aunt had arrived. She was wiping her nose a lot and hugging each of them. Scott kept asking, "Did daddy pick up the pizza yet?" Later in the evening one of the police officers knocked quietly on the door and when Helen pulled the door open, he handed her a pizza. That gesture brought on a fresh torrent of tears from their aunt. She hugged the policeman and Scott did the honors of serving up dinner. They later learned, their dad died in a head-on car collision. The accident altered the lives of three children forever.

Their dad's single sister assumed the role of mother to these young ones. Helen fell into her new position with ease. The children felt loved and secure but missed their daddy desperately. Young Charlene no longer needed to be mother to Annie, instead they loved being able to enjoy each other as sisters. Their aunt never instructed Scott to be the man of the house. They were all allowed to be kids again. She was as fun-loving as dad. Her mothering skills increased daily as they learned to be a family. The four bonded like a mother hen and chicks. Aunt Helen was a gift to these children as much as they were a gift to her.

Annie pulled herself back from those memories. She glanced at the phone again and it dawned on her that Charlie might have an interpretation for the dream. She made a mental note to give her sister a buzz at midmorning break instead of lunch.

* * * *

She pulled into the parking lot at work and entered the building by the side door. Before dropping off her leather laptop case at her desk, she held it close to her face, closed her eyes, and drank in that delicious leather smell. This was a gift to herself two years ago. It was expensive, but she always wanted to own this kind of leather bag. Even though she no longer wrote for a high-powered magazine, she made time to write about lots of other stuff. Maybe that is what gets her into trouble, like with this 'jade'. Annie chided herself, *It's your overactive imagination. Who says things like... mystery adventurer? Duhhhh. No wonder Luke thinks I'm acting goofy lately. Come to think of it, I wonder what's going on in my own head? These awkward feelings have been haunting me lately. Then again, I guess everybody goes through these times in life. Confused. Lack of confidence.*

She made her way to the small break room to grab a cup of coffee. The stupid light was still doing that blinky thing in this tiny room. She jotted a quick post-it note to call the electrician herself. If she kept waiting for her boss to handle this, that light would never get fixed.

The crew of men were outside loading their trucks for the day. This local construction company had been a huge blessing for Annie over the past seven years. Back then, when she came in the door looking for work, she remembered thinking she didn't have the foggiest idea what she was doing there. James, the owner, evidently saw something in her that she did not see in herself. Annie was grateful to scale back from her extremely fast-paced job as a journalist for a Philadelphia magazine and try her hand with this local business.

After seven years, the present job description would include proposal writing and even designing advertisements. James loved the great results those ads brought to his business. A three-day work week was ideal. All those things earned this job its title as "the best job ever". And yet lately, she was unsure why she felt so unsettled.

Today Annie was glad she wore her long-sleeved blouse to divert any comments about a black and blue arm. Her boss already laid out her work for the day. They briefly reviewed the paperwork and swapped some friendly conversation about their families. He informed her of his decision to take a two-week vacation in June. This is the first time he allowed himself more than two or three days off in a row.

James said, "Annie, we can discuss this vacation after I get back from my meeting. I might close the business during those two weeks which means a break for the whole company, including you. We can talk later, I have to run."

Her mind was already planning what to do for two weeks. Luke will love this. He had been trying to get her to take an extended vacation for quite a while. Maybe this was the break she needed to stop all the "gem" stuff.

The morning was busier than usual, and she missed the mid-morning break, so Annie decided to call Charlie at noon. She stepped outside to sit at the picnic bench under the tall shade trees, grabbed the phone, then put it back down to take a deep breath and enjoy the fragrance of spring. Recently she had taken an interest in finding out the names of the shrubs and flowers. It's funny when you're always running with an appointment on your mind, you can miss the little blessings of the day. She bent down to drop the lunch on this side of the table but quickly pulled back before setting it down. The birds had been enjoying the spring days, too. That mess will have to get cleaned off later, for now, she moved to a clean spot.

Swallowing the last of her green tea and putting her feet up on the bench seat, Annie pushed speed dial number two, "Charlie, finally I'm getting a minute to call you. Is everything okay?"

"Oh yes, things are fine. I called earlier about your dream, then I got busy at the house. Now is a perfect time for a phone call."

"Wow Charlie, your morning sounds like it's been as busy as mine. I'm ready for a nap, but an interpretation of that dream should perk me up."

"Okay girl, I'll get right to it. Riding a bike and wearing jeans and sneakers all mean you're in work mode. Your bike is blue because God is giving you some insight in life. Blue represents revelation. He sends someone or some "thing" to wake you up to reveal a truth about yourself. This truth is almost like finding a valuable gem. The green sweater indicates growth and learning how special you are. You will wear that knowledge proudly. God sends an angel to protect you from getting hurt badly."

Annie eked out a quiet, "Wow." *I was glad Charlie could not see my mouth wide open. She knew nothing of the valuable stone I discovered or about an angel young Micah mentioned when I fell off my bike.*

Charlene said, "I'd say the dream is a reminder to trust the Lord. Don't work so hard to figure life out. He's got your back."

"Thanks Charlie, for taking the time to pray about the dream. I'm not quite sure how to trust God more in my life but I'll definitely ask Him. I'm glad I have you for a sister. Thanks for the interpretation, even though I don't fully understand it."

"No worries, Annie. I'm eager to see how this dream plays out in your life."

"Me, too."

"Alright, Sis. Enjoy the rest of your day. I have to go."

Travel Plans

After a busy afternoon at work, James stopped by the office to wrap up his day. He let Annie know the exact dates he planned to close the business. He told her, "I can't pay you in full for those two weeks, but I'd like to give you a bonus as a token of my appreciation for all you do here. You certainly deserve time off."

She lit up, "Thanks, James. I'm sure Luke and I will find a way to enjoy that time.

* * * *

When Luke and Annie finished dinner that evening, she asked him if he'd like to go somewhere on vacation in about seven weeks. He had a puzzled expression and asked, "Did I miss something here?"

"No, I don't think so. I'm pretty sure this is the first time I'm telling you I have two weeks off in June because James is taking a vacation and closing the office."

"Seriously! This is great!" Luke got a faraway look in his eyes as if he were already traveling to some distant place.

Annie interrupted his travels, "So husband, wanna clue me in on where you want to go?"

"Maybe it would be a great chance to go somewhere to practice our Spanish. Now that the big contract is finished at work, it should be pretty easy to leave for a week or so."

She caught his enthusiasm, "Sounds good to me."

"Let's brainstorm and plan quickly because we both know how fast seven weeks is gonna fly by."

"Okay I have off tomorrow. I can run by the travel agency and grab some brochures."

* * * *

Later the next night after several cups of coffee and dozens of brochures they agreed that taking a brisk walk might help them to decide where to vacation. The warm, gentle breeze was a welcome change to leafing through the brochures. The evening was alive with chirping crickets and dancing fireflies.

Annie enjoyed the feel of Luke's fingers intertwined with her own. He said, "This is one of my favorite times of the year."

"Me too. Lately I've been trying to learn some of the names of the shrubs, flowers, and trees. Right now, my favorite is learning about lavender. Did you know besides being so fragrant, it can be eaten and used for health remedies?"

"Eaten! You mean pluck it off the stem and pop it in your mouth raw?"

Annie squeezed his hand, "Maybe you could do that, too. The way I read about it was using the lavender in cookies and scones. Since I'm gonna master the art of baking, one of my first attempts will be the scones."

Luke sighed, "Good job, honey. Keep picturing yourself as a great cook and baker. I can be a very patient man."

She pushed his shoulder and said, "Sooner than you think." She looked aside and mumbled under her breath, "I hope."

Luke was showing off some of his expertise about trees. He pointed out the differences between a white oak and red oak. Annie was impressed.

Their walk took them close to the tree-lined bike path. They went a little further because she wanted to show him the back of Jackson and Emma's house, to point out the spot where she reached through the fence to retrieve the stone. Luke was not enthused.

The clacking of training wheels caught their attention long before Annie realized the Rhineharts were heading their way. Emma gave a squeaky holler, "Yoo-hoo." She responded with a wave. The young boy coasted right up to Luke and said, "I can almost ride this big bike without training wheels. How old were you when you rode a big two-wheeler?"

Luke smiled, "I think you're doing way better than I did at your age."

Micah beamed and then shyly looked at Pops. His grandfather was nodding his head saying, "You are doing fantastic."

Pops extended his hand with a genuine twinkle in his eye, "I am Jackson Rhinehart, this is my lovely wife Emma, and the biker man is Micah."

"Pleased to meet you, sir. I'm Luke Livingston. Thanks for taking care of my Annie when she had her little spill off her bike."

"Well it seemed like the right thing to do since she was bowled over by the stray ball that belonged to our grandson. We sure do know the Lord sometimes orchestrates meetings for His own good purpose."

Emma chimed in, "How is your arm, young lady?"

Extending her arm, "Almost like new."

"Well, Pops just picked up your bike tire today. Do you think he could bring it by your house tomorrow?"

"I have plans for tomorrow but since we are so close to your house could we grab it now. I'm sure my husband could put it back on the bike."

Jackson said, "I'm sure he could, but that would not be completing my end of the bargain. Can I swing by late Saturday morning? It will take me five minutes to put the tire on."

Annie glanced over at Luke and they both said, "That's fine."

Luke continued, "We will both be home handling some yard work. We'll see you then." They said their good-byes and headed back home with the clacking of training wheels fading as they left.

Emma smiled at Jackson and said quietly, "Did you notice how easily Micah approached Annie's husband?"

"I sure did. Maybe time is beginning to heal some deep wounds."

Emma slipped her hand in Jackson's while they finished their evening stroll.

* * * *

Luke and Annie enjoyed the pleasant interruption from pouring over so many travel brochures. Back at the house, they were tidying the table after they finally decided on Mexico. The brochure with white beaches and tall palm trees sat on the top of the pile.

Luke recalled, "Remember in Costa Rica when the howler monkeys scared the living daylights out of us? The locals were stunned 'cause the monkeys usually migrate during the early morning hours not late in the day when we **heard** them."

Annie shook her head, catching Luke's excitement, "Yeah, that was amazing!"

He continued, "What a treat to hear them so close to us. The only people who got a good look at them were the little boy and his brother who stood on the rooftop of that cute little restaurant. They rattled off in Spanish so fast and I could only catch two words. Actually, only one, monos (monkeys)."

"It was a bummer we didn't get a good look at them, but we heard their fog horn calls echoing in the dry trees."

Luke gestured with his hands cupped up at his face, "Hence the name, Howler Monkeys."

They imitated the screech together.

Luke said, "Now, I'm getting excited for this trip. Might be fun to spot some unusual wildlife in Mexico."

"Sounds like a plan. I'll call the travel agent tomorrow."

Annie thought, *this will give me a vacation from my grandiose visions of an expensive green stone.*

* * * *

Saturday, mid-morning, Annie heard the truck and peeked out from under her wide-brimmed straw hat. She saw Jackson pull up to the house in the truck with Micah in the passenger seat. Annie stood up from the newly planted lavender and stepped around the purple crocuses and happy-faced daffodils. Luke was turning over the soil in the vegetable garden area. He had finished driving a dozen tall stakes for the tomato plants deep into the ground. He was tying the last of the white cotton string for the green beans to climb, when Pops pulled up. Luke brushed his hands against his jeans and made his way toward the truck. He whistled a long, low sound of admiration as he approached the visitors. “Wow, Jackson, that is in excellent shape. Is it a '68?"

"Sounds like you know something about trucks."

"My knowledge is very limited. My older brother loves cars and trucks. I learned from him."

"Okay. This is a 1968 Chevy C/K 10 series. She carries a V8 engine and she runs like a top for her age."

Luke said, "Do ya mind if I take a peek under the hood?"

Jackson popped the hood and narrated, "She has a 350-cubic inch V8 with a new serpentine belt drive. Time deteriorated the previous belt but now she hums. There is an AM/FM radio with a CD stereo. I have to admit I like that upgrade. So does my buddy here!"

Luke said, "Sweeeet!"

Jackson added jokingly, "The shiny silver color does not reflect my docile side it speaks of my flashy wild side."

Luke responded, "So… this is a glimpse of your wild side. I'm diggin' it."

They exchanged friendly glances.

Micah was standing next to Jackson waiting for the truck exchange to finish. As the guys talked, Annie got her bike from the garage. She wheeled it slowly as she held up the front end without the tire.

Jackson turned to his grandson, "Are you okay, little guy?"

"Sure, Pops."

"Well then how 'bout if you get the bicycle tire for me from the back of the truck. Be careful climbing up there."

Micah wasted no time as he jogged to the back saying, "Pops, I 'member how you showed me to use the bumper like a ladder to get up."

He scrambled into the bed of the truck and held up the tire triumphantly. Luke said, "Good job, buddy". Then he wrestled it off the back of the truck and handed it to Luke. He hopped down, grabbed the tire, and ran it over to Jackson.

Pops turned the bike over and mounted the new tire onto the bike with the efficiency of a Nascar mechanic. It prompted Annie to ask, "What work did you do before you retired? Were you a car mechanic?"

"No, my expertise was not with cars. I enjoy tinkering mechanically, but I was a physician for thirty-five years. We had a small family practice located about fifteen miles from here. So, I guess you can say I am still fixing things," he replied laughingly.

Annie mused, *funny how we assume things about people. Come to think of it, I can see how he would've been a very caring doctor. He's soft spoken and assesses situations with such ease.* She said, "I think you must have been a very good doctor."

"Thank you, Annie. How's that arm?"

"Much better. Emma did a good job bandaging me up."

Jackson nodded his head, "Yes, she has done her share of bandaging in her lifetime."

His response made Annie wonder where Micah's parents were. She had an uneasy feeling in the pit of her stomach. Could this kid have experienced some stuff like she had when she was a child. She tried to rope in her thoughts before they took off like a runaway train. She felt Jackson's hand on her arm, "Are you okay?"

She shook off the memories and said, "Oh, sorry. Yep, I'm good."

Jackson was not too convinced. He turned around to find the little guy digging in the dirt.

He stood up and held up a large worm, "Hey, Pops, it's easy to get worms in this dirt."

Jackson said, "Son, you need to get permission before you dig on someone else's property."

Micah sheepishly replied, "Sorry."

Luke spoke up, "You must be able to get bait quickly when you go fishing."

The boy looked up at Jackson and smiled, "We love to fish, but the thing is... we never catch anything."

"Well, your luck is about to change. I own a small Boston Whaler and we keep it at the city dock. Would you guys like to go fishing with me around three o'clock this afternoon? That would give me enough time to finish prepping this garden area for my wife. Lately, I can't find fishing buddies since everybody's busy with their yards and their kids."

Micah looked pleadingly at Pops. He just smiled and said, "I am sure Emma could pack us some sandwiches and snacks. We'll meet you back here at three. Thank you, Luke." Jackson firmly shook his hand.

"Sure thing. Thanks for the bike repair. See you guys back here in a couple hours. Luke watched the two climb up into Jackson's 'wild side' vehicle and smiled. He saluted them and returned to his work.

Annie smiled as she heard her husband whistling while he dragged the rake through the stubborn weeds.

Fishing Buddies

As Jackson pulled into the driveway, the boy jumped out and ran towards Emma, "Lita, Lita, we're going fishing wif Luke. He has a boat and he needs some buddies to go wif him. He's gonna help us catch fish this time."

He ran upstairs and left Emma standing with her mouth slightly open, "Was that you, Micah? Or did some super kid fly up those stairs?" She turned to Jackson as he was coming in the door. "What's going on? That child has not been this excited since, well, I don' t know when."

He squeezed Emma, "It looks like our new friend has a boat, and he wants us to be his fishing pals this afternoon. We are going to meet him at three to catch some dinner."

"Mmm, fresh fish. It makes my mouth water just thinking about it. I'll get busy preparing some side dishes to have with our meal. So, dear, make sure you stop at the fish market on First Street before you come home because we all know what kind of fishermen you two really are."

"Oh, ye of little faith," Jackson taunted. "Emma, would you mind making some sandwiches for us? I'm gonna gather some tackle and bait before we head back to Luke's."

"I'm two steps ahead of you, Jackson Rhinehart. I made some chicken salad a little while ago. I'll whip up some sandwiches and throw a few other goodies together. I'm so glad I went to the grocery store yesterday. Just give me a good reason to feed some hungry men and I'm one happy camper."

Emma whistled as she busied herself in the kitchen. She stopped long enough to hear Jackson humming in the garage too. She shook her head and grinned. Slamming drawers caught her attention from upstairs. Emma interrupted her food prep to peek in on her grandson. She giggled to see so many clothes laid out on the bed including a raincoat and boots.

"Honey, do you think you'll need all those clothes to go fishing?"

"I don't know, I never fished from a boat, Lita."

"Maybe I can help you. You'll need a sweatshirt. I don't think you'll need boots."

"But, Lita, every time I see the men on TV go fishing, they have big boots on and rain coats."

She squeezed her sweet boy. "Well, maybe Luke won't mind if you bring your rain gear."

After some discussion about clothes, he continued to look over his final choices. Emma went downstairs and left him to finish his packing. He decided to wear his rain boots and carry his jacket, so he wouldn't have to stuff them in the backpack. He put his green and red sweater on the bed.

Micah climbed up on his bed and held the sweater up to his nose and sniffed it. "Mommy and Daddy, you're comin' wif me on my first boat trip. I'm gonna wear this sweater you got me from Cow-ombia even if it's little on me. Remember how I told ya me and Pops can't catch fish? Luke said our luck is changing today. I forgot to tell you 'bout Luke; he's our new friend. You'll like him. He shares his things just like you guys always told me to share. Mommy, Luke has Annie. She has yellow hair like yours. She is not as purty as you, Mommy. When I see her, I know she's a good lady 'cause her angel is always wif her. I'm gonna catch my first fish from the boat today. Daddy, sorry you can't be there, but you can watch. You'll be proud of me."

He struggled into his sweater as he continued, "Mommy and Daddy, come on. I want ya to see the look on Pop's face when I catch a BIG fish." He pulled the sweater down and buried his nose in it one more time and took a deep breath. Then he grabbed his full backpack, boots, and rain jacket and hurried out to the garage to help Pops.

Seeing his grandson in that sweater caught him off guard, and Jackson needed some air. He stood outside the garage as Micah chattered. He stepped back in to put his arm around the precious boy. They carefully went over their choice of tackle at least three times. They settled on the two-ounce dipsies. Jackson suggested they bring some red and orange rubber worms too. Micah agreed and reached into the tackle box and lifted a bucktail out carefully. "Pops, what do ya' think? Can we bring this too?"

"Perfect. I remember reading about some anglers catching flounder with worms and bucktail."

"Okay then, should we bring the green and yellow one?"

"Sure, let's bring both bucktails and hope for some fish that love bright colors."

"Pops, I think today is gonna be our lucky fishing day 'cause Luke said so."

"I agree, Son. Now I think we have enough supplies."

"Oh no, Pops, we don't wanna forget." He ran out to the side garden with his little tin bucket. He came back with four fat, squiggly worms.

"If you can catch fish like you catch worms, we'll have plenty of fish for dinner."

Micah smiled proudly.

Now they just had to wait two hours until three o'clock came around. They headed into the house to grab a snack. They both wanted to save their sandwiches for the boat since Pops mentioned that eating on the boat is part of the fun.

* * * *

Luke greeted his fishing pals out front and helped them load their gear into his truck. He saw the young boy's huge armful of clothes and said, "Good job. As fishermen, we have to be prepared. By the way, I like your boots."

Micah stood a little taller, "Thanks. I'm ready to catch fish."

The two men grinned and kept loading the truck for the trip.

Annie came out of the house with a small bag. She handed it to Micah, "Looks like you've got plenty of stuff for the trip, but I hoped you might enjoy this bag of Twizzlers. My husband seems to think these licorice stick candies bring him luck on a fishing trip."

Timidly, he reached for the bag and thanked Annie.

The three men waved good-bye as they pulled out of the driveway. She smiled at the sight of what looked like three little boys on Christmas morning. She shook her head and hopped on her bike for a much-needed stretch.

* * * *

Captain Luke eased the boat out into the bay because he sensed his young visitor's nervousness. Pops was pointing out the egrets and the blue herons along the marshes. He asked Micah, "Doesn't it look like an invisible paintbrush was coloring those tall marsh grasses a beautiful shade of green?"

Squirming uneasily, he answered, "Maybe the marshes are drinking green water from a straw." They all chuckled. The men saw the boy slowly inching away from his Pops. After a few more minutes of gaining his sea legs, Micah was spotting buoys, boats, and a few more egrets. By the time they anchored, he was feeling quite at home on the boat.

Luke said, "Looks like we're ready. Can you put the worm on the bucktail?"

The worm digger had no problem handling those creatures he dug up at the house. He threaded the wigglers onto the hook like a pro. Pops watched him with pride in his eyes.

Luke said, "Sometimes the worm dies pretty quickly in salt water, but I've seen men catch some keepers even if the bait dies. I think threading them close to the bucktail kinda tricks the fish into taking the bait. Besides, if you can catch fish like you handle worms, we'll be in for a good day."

The grandfather and boy smiled at each other, shrugged their shoulders and got busy baiting their lines. Luke looked from one to the other, "Hmm, did I miss somethin'?"

* * * *

They each picked a spot in the boat to stand and cast their lines into the water. Pops made sure his grandson was only a grip away from him. The boy's dipsy sunk quickly to the bay's muddy bottom. Micah instinctively gave the line some little tugs. Pops spent more time praying the boy would have the victory of at least one keeper.

Only a few minutes passed when the youngest angler said, "I think I have something." Luke encouraged him to hold the reel firmly and occasionally yank it back enough to create a slight slack in the line. The more he reeled the line, the harder it became to wind it in. Micah looked to Pops for a nod of approval to keep reeling. Jackson winked.

The captain positioned his fishing net over the side of the boat and said, "I can see your fish." He lowered his voice to keep the boy focused, "Keep reeling a little more. Slow. Slow. Steady."

Little arms strained with each turn of the reel as the net scooped under the flounder and dropped it into the cockpit. He released his grip, shook his tired arms, and bent close to his catch. Pops offered, "Do ya' need any help?"

"I think I can get it, Pops."

The child smiled gratefully at his grandfather, then turned to work on the hook. Pops swatted at the greenheads that gathered around them. The pungent smell of the bait attracted those insects quickly. Before Jackson could even swat at the second round of pests, Micah stood up triumphantly holding the hook that came out of the fish's mouth. He shouted, "Got it!" He added, "I think it's a keeper."

Luke nodded, "No doubt about it. It's a keeper. You did a great job getting that hook out."

Pops agreed wholeheartedly.

Luke grabbed the measuring stick and said, "How 'bout if you guys hold the fish so I can get a quick measurement." They struggled with the slippery fish and shrieked with delight when the size was called out, "Fourteen inches, that's a solid catch for a winter fluke!" Luke was grinning from ear-to-ear. Jackson helped stow the flounder in the box below the deck. They covered the catch with ice. The youngest boatman slid the lock securely making sure his keeper would not escape.

Jackson could already picture the fish sitting on the turkey platter on their dining room table. Emma had a way with cooking food to perfection and presenting it with flare. He even smiled to himself as he recalled they did not have a platter that was designated as a 'fish' platter.

"Can we do that again? Maybe Pops can catch the next one." They all laughed as they got right back to their positions and dropped their lines. The captain was grateful for the breeze because those flies could make or break an afternoon of fishing. He hauled in the next keeper which narrowly met the legal requirements. Micah's was the biggest catch of the day. Jackson caught one, but they had to throw the small catch back. The boy shouted to the fish, "We'll be back for you when you get bigger."

He turned to Luke, "I think we better eat some licorice, so we can tell Annie they gave us good luck."

"Oh my gosh, I forgot all about our Twizzlers. Jackson, can you get us each a soda?"

The doctor followed orders. They each raised a can, then sipped their sodas through their Twizzler straws as a celebration toast. With a mischievous smile after a long sip, Micah threw his head back, and burped out, "What a day!"

Luke howled and Jackson shook his head, *these two are gonna be good friends.*

* * * *

Luke docked the boat as they gathered their gear and said jokingly, "If you think that was fun, wait 'til I teach you how to fillet those fish."

Grandfather and grandson stepped off the boat and headed to the sink on the dock. Micah started to unzip his life jacket. Jackson said, "Whoa there, that stays on until we get 'on the hard'."

"Um, I thought this dock was the hard."

"No. 'The hard' is an expression for the land not the hard dock."

"Oh, now I get it."

The captain strolled toward the sink. He turned his cap backwards, so he'd have a clear view to slice and dice. Pops already grabbed the stool so the five-year-old could step up and get a good look at the whole process. Luke warned, "A fillet knife is very sharp, so I'm gonna let you watch this time. When you get a little bigger, you'll get a chance to do this all by yourself."

"I just wanna carry the fish when it's time to give 'em to my Lita."

"That's a great idea." He held the fish steady on the cutting board and began to swipe the scaling knife across it's back several times. The sticky scales came off easily as he ran water over the fish. He proceeded to insert the knife just below the gills to make the two slices that looked like the top of a 'Y'. Afterwards, he cut methodically down the spine and along the top of the bone as if there were invisible dotted lines. The 'Y' cut was complete. He slid the knife just under the meat along the back and sliced outward being careful to avoid any bones. He did the same on the other side of the fish. The guests were amazed how easily the four pieces of fillet were removed from the flounder leaving only a skeleton with a head attached.

"That is so cool!"

Luke discarded the waste in the trashcan on the side of the sink, rinsed the fillets, and placed them in a bag. "Even though I'm good at this, please chew slowly when you eat them 'cause it's easy to miss a stray bone."

"That looked like one of the nicest surgeries I have ever seen." Jackson playfully tousled his grandson's hair as more ice got dumped on the fillets before tying the bag. After the trash was wrapped tightly, it was placed in the trashcan with a brick on top. The gulls circling above flew away when the brick was laid. Luke turned to the five-year-old and handed the catch to him like a gold medal. Micah stood tall and accepted the bag with a grin. He looked up to the sky and slightly lifted his fish saying, "See, I told ya." His smile faded as he wiped his nose and a few tears onto his sweater. The men understood those gestures were a salute to the child's parents.

The boy placed the fish in his own cooler when Luke said, "Now you can wash down the boat." Micah skipped to get the hose and started squirting every last inch of the boat while the men rearranged and secured the lines from the boat to the dock. They kept ducking to avoid a few drenching squirts from the excited sprayer.

When the boat was secured and cleaned, Jackson shook Luke's hand, "I can't thank you enough for a great day. Now, how 'bout next week, you and Annie come over for some of Emma's great cooking?"

Luke smiled and looked over his shoulder as if someone might be listening. "Sounds good to me. It's funny that Annie's sister Charlene is such a good cook, yet, my wife missed out on that talent. She's ready to learn, but kinda misses the mark. She does get an 'A' for effort. Jackson, your wife Emma sounds like a regular chef."

"Yes, sir, she is quite gifted."

"I'll check with Annie's schedule and let you know for sure when we can make it for dinner."

Jackson noticed how proud Luke was of his wife for trying. Annie was deeply loved and respected by her husband. Pops liked what he was learning about this man, his new friend. He couldn't help but think, what a good dad he will be some day.

When the three of them got back to Luke's house, Micah pulled the cooler into Pop's truck and onto his lap. He waved excitedly and shouted, "Thanks, Luke, that was so much fun. I can't wait to see Lita's face when she sees this!"

When they were pulling out of the driveway, Luke waved and said, "Enjoy your dinner. I'll keep in touch."

A Challenging Dream

It was a lovely afternoon for a bike ride. Annie chuckled as she remembered Luke telling his stories two nights ago about the fishing trip with Jackson and Micah. *He has not laughed like that in a long time.*

He even took two huge swigs of soda in order to demonstrate the burping episode with his little buddy. He also told her it was Micah who said, "We better get the Twizzlers, so we can tell Annie they gave us good luck."

"Really, Luke? He said that?"

"Yep. He's a different kind of kid. Thoughtful or something. I can't describe it. He's just cool."

She liked the sparkle in Luke's eyes when he spoke about their fishing adventures. Or was it just being with the boy? Well, in any case, Luke was certainly having fun.

As Annie pedaled, the sunlight flickered on the diamond ring on her finger. She smiled as she could picture Luke bending on one knee in the wet sand at the beach five years ago. It wasn't supposed to rain that day and Luke said he couldn't wait any longer to propose. When Annie said yes, Luke jumped up to hug her, dropped the ring and they spent an hour trying to find it. It rained so hard and they were drenched but neither would give up. Rain eventually washed the mud into little rivers on the beach. She was glad for the rain, in a way, because it hid the streams of tears that were making muddy tracks on her cheeks. The puddles on the beach formed mini pools which made it almost impossible to locate the ring. Then one of the streams was redirected by a gnarled oyster shell. They spotted the ring at the same time, resting along the shell's jagged edge. Luke scooped it up before it sank into the mire again. He quickly put it on her finger, then Annie stooped down to pocket the oyster that saved the day.

Remembering that scene warmed her heart. She knew beyond a shadow of a doubt, even if they never found the engagement ring, she and Luke would be together. She absently twirled the ring on her left finger and noticed how the two bands of white gold fit so perfectly together. The sparkling pear-shaped diamond was stunning. It symbolized love between her and Luke. Maybe the value of her green gem was just like the diamond. Annie was not sure what the green rock symbolized but she was eager to uncover its mystery.

"Lord, what could You possibly be saying to me through a green gem?"

* * * *

Annie coasted into the driveway and parked her bike next to the shed on the side of Ray and Charlene's house. Her sister's whistling was coming from the kitchen.

The creaky sound of the back door heralded her arrival, "Good afternoon, Sis."

"Annie, thanks for coming to help. How's the arm?"

Raising her arm slightly, "Healing quickly. Only a hint of black and blue."

"Hey, it looks so much better."

"Onto more important matters, what's on the menu today, Charlie?"

"Well, if you can help me grate some carrots, I can make the official Aunt Sally pineapple-carrot nut breads. Otherwise, they have to be only pineapple nut breads since the carrots are too hard for me to grate."

"Ask no more." She helped herself to a cup of coffee and got busy grating carrots. The sisters fell into an ease with each other and chatted about the men and kids. As long as Charlene directed, Annie did well in the kitchen. She shredded two pounds of carrots and proudly wore orange hands as evidence that she actually was baking. Charlie barely glanced at the recipe which left Annie a little jealous and always amazed.

The jealousy quickly dissipated as Annie saw her sister smoothly lean on her crutch to free her hands and add several eggs to the batter. She volunteered to start the Kitchen Aid and slowly added the ingredients as Charlene instructed.

The next job was to grease the mini loaf pans. She casually asked, "So how do you do this part when you're solo?"

Charlie replied, "Lots of planning ahead. Usually Liz greases the pans for me and drapes them with linen towels. Mark shreds carrots or chops nuts and leaves them in easy-slide Ziploc bags. Ray bought these great canisters for flour and sugar that are very simple to open, even for me."

"Sounds like team work."

Annie told her how James surprised her with the business shutting down for two weeks. She loved watching the expression on her sister's face when she told her they were taking a trip to Mexico. They were like little girls again. High fiving and yahooing. The amazing thing about Charlie is her sincerity. Even though she has had to adjust to so many changes as she adapts to MS, she is always excited when the other guy gets fun surprises. She does not have a jealous bone in her body.

They were working diligently assembling the breads when they heard a commotion outside. Both headed toward the door. When Charlene swung it open, they saw three local teenagers carting wheelbarrows, shovels, and rakes to the back of the house. Charlie exclaimed, "It's the teens! They're here to weed and mulch some of the flower beds."

She welcomed them exuberantly. They waved and greeted the sisters. The one young man reminded Charlie this was the date she picked to get help with the yard work.

Charlene told them she was concerned about it getting to be so late in the day. They assured her they would be done before dark. They got to work with music blasting.

"Charlene, when we were growing up, did we **ever** stop to consider other people besides ourselves?"

"I really can't remember helping others too much. We were too busy trying to survive. Our lives were quite different back then, Sis."

"Well, you and Ray are great role models. Your husband's a sweetheart. Ever since the two of you began dating, he's been like a brother to me. Now your kids and their friends are following your good example of looking out for the other guy."

"Annie, our kids look up to you and Luke like a second set of parents. Are you **sure** you don't see yourself as a parent?"

"Come on, Sis, let's not start that again."

"What are you so afraid of?" As soon as Charlie asked the question, she saw the vein on the side of Annie's neck pop. The next words were sure to be heated ones.

"Are you serious, Charlene?" Annie stood up to pace.

"Do ya' want me to name a few dozen reasons why I should not have kids."

Charlie stood to face her eye-to-eye, "I'm not trying to pick a fight. As your big sister, I'm trying to get you to see the truth about yourself. You would be a good mom, Annie."

She rolled her eyes, "I am not like you, Charlene. Bouncing back from struggles or finding the good in everything. That's not me. That is **you**, dear sister. Those genes did **not** make it to me. They got snuffed out before I came along, or when mother decided she no longer wanted to be there for her little girls."

Charlie winced at that remark. “Annie, that’s **not** fair. Mom suffered far more than we knew. Remember Aunt Helen telling us about so many of mom’s struggles with depression. Maybe that generation didn’t know there were medicines to help deal with mental disorders.”

“Charlie, no offense, but you have your head in the sand. Our mother did **not** care about us, she cared about herself. Three helpless little kids never meant enough for her to deal with her issues. Our dad deserved a better wife and a better life. Instead he had to shoulder the burden of her wackiness and then the job of raising us by himself.”

“Ouch, Annie. She is not here to give her side of the story.”

“EXACTLY! She left. She chose **not** to be here. And frankly, we were probably better off without her.”

“Hey, instead of looking at what you call a bad example, can you think of any good mothers?”

“No way! Don’t lay the guilt on me right now. Maybe I need to blow off some steam. Some of the issues I’m dealing with lately have everything to do with us as kids… and me not wanting to have any.”

“Annie, what issues?

“Nothing. Never mind.”

Charlie plopped down in the chair to steady herself. Now her own mind was reeling. *Is she referring to depression? What issues is she talking about? I better approach this subject with caution.* “Okay, Annie, I’m all ears if you need to get something off your chest.”

“Nope. You’re not a shrink. I don’t need a therapist or whatever it is you’re doing. I’m gonna go home before I say things I might regret.”

“Aw, come on, Annie. I’m your sister, not a shrink, not a doctor. Besides, **sisters** are definitely more qualified to lend an ear than those people with lots of letters after their names.”

That comment helped the younger sister calm down.

Annie looked sad and replied, "You know you are the best mother. And Aunt Helen did a great job of filling a hole in my heart ever since I was a little girl. She must have had a million ways to make me happy. Remember her quoting Proverbs 17:22?"

They chanted together, "A joyful heart is good medicine, but a broken spirit dries up the bones."

At that Charlie giggled, "Yeah, Aunt Helen made sure we experienced the joyful part. Remember when she let us have that bubble-blowing contest in the house?"

"Yeah and soap was all over the floor when Scott came running in from outside. He slipped on the floor and slid all the way to the back hall. After we knew he was okay, the game changed from bubble-blowing to slip and slide on the soap drenched floors."

"Aunt Helen said we did not need a bath that night, she took us out back and hosed us down as we ran and screeched until our bellies hurt."

"Charlie, you did it again. I don't know how you take a tense situation and turn it around." Annie flopped onto the rocking chair and started to cry, "I could never be a mom like you or Aunt Helen. And I don't want to be a mom like our mother."

"Shh, baby sister. I believe God's timing is perfect. When you're ready, you'll know it. Don't worry. I'm sorry if I pushed you. Shh. For now, go on being the greatest aunt for my kids."

Charlene smoothed Annie's hair and the sadness melted away with each stroke down her blonde locks. Annie marveled at how Charlene diffused the outburst. The annoying thumping in her head kept playing the tune of 'unworthy' in her ears, and it prevented her from considering how to follow Charlene's pattern of handling difficulties. *Heck, I'm not even sure what I'm unworthy of. Whatever it is, it makes me feel bad. I need a break from the tug-o-war in my head. I'm not sure pursuing a green gem has anything to do with discovering something about myself. But, if it does, I want to be quick about it. My sister's right, I need a vacation!*

* * * *

The teens outside were just wrapping up their lawn work, so Charlene offered them iced tea and fresh baked pineapple-carrot-nut bread. Three breads and dozens of glasses of iced tea disappeared. "Yikes, is that normal to scoff food like that?" Annie shrieked after the kids left.

Charlene's eyes twinkled as she gave a shrug.

It didn't take long for Annie to realize she was going to have to stay longer to help bake some more breads.

Charlie got a little pensive during the next round of baking. Annie probed, "So, is it your turn to cry and pout about not having life figured out? Or is something keeping you up at night you might want to discuss?"

"Funny you should ask. Two nights ago, I had a dream and you were the star. But honestly, this doesn't feel like a good time to talk about dreams."

"Charlie, maybe I need to hear it. Who knows? Maybe it can help me."

"Okay, kiddo, here it is. A little girl is skipping and playing in a beautiful field dotted with an amazing display of flowers. The flowers had their own personality and the grass was as soft as a plush carpet. A child is playing hide-n-seek with a knight. They're having such fun running and giggling together. The little girl trips and the knight picks her up. They hug and laugh. The last time the little girl trips, she falls asleep. She is awakened by the sharp stinging of bumble bees. "Ouch. Ouch." She looks around to find the knight, but he is gone. The little girl lays her head down and falls asleep again until the sensation of falling jolts her awake. This time she finds herself on top of a large mound of sand. She's older now. The sand begins to shake and slides her off the dune. She jumps to her feet and begins running to play with some floating bubbles. There are some little kids playing bubbles with her."

Annie asked, "You have an interpretation for **that**?"

Charlene answered, "Yes, I do."

"First of all, how do ya know it's me in the dream?"

"Well, I sense it in my gut especially because the little one in the dream is wearing your childhood hat with white lace. Remember it?"

"You mean the pink one with the beautiful lace woven around the crest? The one I sometimes refused to take off during dinner? My favorite piece of clothing even when I went to bed?"

"Yep, that's the one."

"I loved it. Wait! I'm wearing it in the dream?"

Charlie bobbed her head slowly.

Annie stood sluggishly and looked pale, "Actually, Charlene, some of the dream seems obvious to me. I wanna hear what your interpretation is but you're gonna have to give me a minute." She excused herself and went to the powder room.

When she returned she had red eyes and a puffy face.

Charlene saw the expression and stalled to give her sister time to get composed, "Annie, can you put these breads on the window sill to cool down before I wrap them up. Then we can go sit on the porch." They each grabbed a glass of water and headed out back.

Annie sat on the sofa and patted the cushion next to her, "I think I'm ready."

She leaned on her sister's shoulder as Charlene began, "When you were a little girl, you loved being with your knight in shining armor. When he disappeared, lots of doubts attacked you like stinging bees. As the sands of time moved forward and you got older, you saw life from a more mature perspective. For a while, your outlook prevented you from playing and skipping lightheartedly. Then something jolts you to a new, carefree view of life allowing fun to enter again."

At the end of the interpretation both Annie and Charlene were crying. They held each other and sobbed. The dream hit home for both women. They would still occasionally mourn dad's tragic death. It was a long time ago when Annie was seven, Scott was nine, and Charlie was twelve. His death set all of them reeling for several years. Tender, caring friends helped the young family push through the hard times.

Clinging to each other, they each remembered the struggles of that part of life. Maturity taught them to grow and accept loss. Annie sensed she needed to let go of some things from the past. Maybe this dream was a gentle reminder that it's time to bury some pain-filled memories and not allow fear of death or losing someone steal the great times to be enjoyed right now.

Annie said, "I thought I **did** leave a serious part of my life when I left the magazine."

Charlene responded, "You left the pressures of the magazine and that was good. Maybe God has another thing in store for you so can enjoy life even more. You know the second half of John 10:10 says, "I came that they might have life, and might have it abundantly."

"I don't remember those verses as quickly as you do. I do know besides grieving over daddy again, I've been searching for something lately. I'm not sure what **it** is. I probably need to schedule more times to have fun." They laughed at the way Annie even looked at having to **schedule** fun into her day.

"Little sister, sometimes grieving happens in stages. Look at us two grown women crying over our daddy who has been gone for many years. It's okay to be sad, even over something from long ago. Healing happens in waves. If we don't stay under that wave, we can come up, inhale, and enjoy life again."

Annie got quiet and asked, "Charlie, I feel like a mess. I didn't think I had so many struggles until recently. The bike accident started things off. Then came my dream on the bike with the green sweater, and now your dream. Is God telling me I'm a mess."

"Sometimes He lets us see ourselves **in** a mess. Not that we are a mess, but we know when things in life are messy. I've found when He puts the pieces of our puzzling lives together, He fits them together perfectly. Annie, do your part, leave the rest in His capable hands."

"Charlie, you seem to handle things with... well, I guess the word I'm looking for is grace. I wish I could do it like you do."

"Sis, for some reason you seem to be putting a lot of pressure on yourself. Looks like a trip is exactly what you need. Go away and enjoy time with Luke. If I were you, I wouldn't even bother to learn Spanish. Go and enjoy the change of scenery!"

"You have a nice way of putting things."

She gathered her things and grabbed a bread for Luke. He would never forgive her if she came home empty-handed after baking with Charlene. She held up her bread, "I think Luke will enjoy this delicious bread with some jelly. I might even serve it as tonight's dinner."

"Oh, Annie, at least you still have a sense of humor."

She gave Charlene a hollow smile with a slight shrug of her shoulder, secretly wishing she was kidding about the bread for dinner.

The Prayer Meeting

Emma was thinking about how much she cherished this unique group of women and the times they've shared together every Tuesday for nearly thirty years. They held hands, offered tissues, visited family members in hospitals, and recently even had to attend a funeral for one member of this special group. Emma was one who prayed a lot but seldom requested prayers for herself.

She started off, "Well, girls, every day I have several opportunities to exercise muscles I thought were toned and strong. I'm referring to the muscle called 'patience'. It seems the Lord knew I needed a major work-out to strengthen it."

"When Rebecca was a child, if my memory serves me correctly, there were many times for me to exercise patience." The other ladies giggled remembering what it was like raising their own children. Emma continued, "When I reflect on my new station in life, some things have become clear to me. When I stood up from tending my garden last week, the old bones objected. I stretched and bent a few extra times to get the blood flowing. I was remembering as a young mom tending to my garden when I did not need to stretch to accomplish the task at hand. It occurred to me, besides being young, I was incredibly active. I did not run marathons or join local fund-raising jogs. Laundry, cooking, mending clothes, food shopping, gardening, and caring for my daughter and Jackson kept me very occupied. My patience was constantly exercised. It was a rock-solid muscle, so to speak. When Rebecca and Tim would visit with Micah, it was sheer joy to be with them. The burden of parenting was Rebecca and Tim's. I got the chance to enjoy their little family. The only patience I needed was to withhold my words of wisdom from Rebecca. I was navigating my way as grandmother while Rebecca was discovering her own way as a mother.

Now times have changed. My responses to situations are not very kind. Just last week, Micah literally pulled a muddy cat across the carpet and into the kitchen to announce that 'Boots', our neighbor's cat, needed a bath. I am no longer observing his sweet childish antics. Now I must clean up the mess and teach him right from wrong. By the way, it's quite amazing how much mud can come off a drenched cat. My beautiful gray and gold carpet is slightly darker despite three shampoos."

Susan stood up and placed her arm lightly on her friend's shoulder and handed her a tissue.

Emma said, "Even though I'd like to cry, I wanna get the rest of this story out. Please, Susan, let me say this before I get too choked up."

She gave her a little squeeze and sat down.

Emma sighed deeply and continued, "Unfortunately, things are not quite so cute any more. My heart misses Rebecca and Tim desperately and longs for carefree grandmother interaction, which does not require an abundance of patience, only laughs and hugs. Needless to say, since my patience has not had continuous daily exercise, as it did when I was a full-time parent, it's not as strong as it used to be. Now, girls, I think it's safe to say I know you pretty well. I do **not** want you to pray for patience for me because we all know when we pray like that, the Lord gives us opportunities for that muscle to grow. I have plenty of those opportunities. I'd like prayers for my perspective to change; for things not to ruffle my feathers so much. I want to have fun with my grandson which is just as important as teaching him to be responsible. I need to celebrate my flip-flopped station in life since it went from mom to grandmom and now back to mom again. I'm very tired."

The small group hovered around Emma like hens around a sickly chick. They hugged and comforted her. Susan spoke up, "Girls, I have something to say. Can y'all sit down for a minute?"

These friends knew the wisdom Susan carried, so they eagerly sat to listen but they remained in a tight circle around Emma.

Susan cleared her throat, "This is not a time for us to fall back into some bad habits." All the girls shifted uneasily. She continued, "I agree with Emma when she says she needs prayer for her perspective to change about this situation. We've learned over the years about some 'old adages' and how false they are. God doesn't use tough situations in our lives to see if He can show us our lack of patience. He doesn't beat us over the head and say, "I told you so". Emma, I don't think God is testing to see if you use your 'patience muscle', as you put it. I believe He's reminding you that patience is a part of His expression of love.

It's a good idea for all of us to recognize Emma's weariness. Which means it's a good time to remember that His Word says in Matthew 11:28, "Come to Me, all who are weary and heavy-laden, and I will give you rest."

Emma, you came to the right place to ask for help. We don't need to pray for patience or even more kindness or anything that we think we're lacking. How about if we concentrate on who our Lord is? Let's remind ourselves that His supply is greater than any of our needs. We can rally in a prayer of strength and not of neediness. Let's not pray for patience because we're afraid of what might happen. Instead, let's agree with God's Word, we already have patience because it's a part of His love."

Not surprisingly, Emma was the first to stand up. "Wow. I needed that reminder." She turned to the group, "Susan's right. I've been so tired I began to believe the lie that God would send me more trials in order to strengthen me. Those thoughts made me even more weary. I'm covered in God's love and that means I have all the patience and kindness I need because I have Him."

One of the ladies suggested they pray as the Lord had been teaching them. "Let's pray prayers of faith and not fear. Then we can watch and see how God will help and direct Emma and Jackson in these difficult times. He will be there for this family."

* * * *

After prayer, they enjoyed some desserts and coffee. Emma's dear friend offered her an unusual looking muffin. Emma bit the muffin and her eyes lit up, "This is delicious. Just the right amount of sweet. I think I taste one or two unusual flavors, too. Yum."

Susan said, "Yep, it's an oldie but goodie. It's a family recipe of banana French toast and it's baked in a muffin tin instead of on a skillet. And you're right, there is an extra ingredient. It's rather fun-tasting, don't you think?"

Emma squinted, looked at her friend, and asked, "You're not only talking about this muffin are you, Susan?"

"No, I'm not. My friend, your role has changed but **you** don't have to change. Maybe if you adjust some of the ways you deal with your grandson, you'll enjoy him more than you have been able to lately. You're still Micah's grandma, **not** his mom. Sure, he needs extra guidance and some discipline, but you do not have to do it as Rebecca would have." She gestured to the muffin, "You're an oldie but goodie too. God will show you how to give Micah what he needs seasoned with an extra measure of wisdom. Micah's a sweet, young boy with a tender heart. He misses his mom and dad, but you are not replacing them. I think it would be sad for Micah if he had to miss the carefree fun ways of his Lita, too. You can find creative ways to come alongside the little guy, just like the French toast with a new twist. It might be more enjoyable for both of you."

Teary-eyed, Emma gave Susan a firm squeeze as she whispered, "Oldie but goodie, huh? I've heard **that** before. Didn't you just teach us to watch out for those old sayings?"

Susan added, "Yeah, but this one's true. Unlike the one that says be careful when you pray for patience, as if Our Father in heaven is waiting to clobber us with all kinds of tests to see if we've finally become patient. Nonsense!

Anyhow, what do ya think of that muffin?"

Emma tasted another bite and gave a thumbs up.

After another sip of coffee, Emma told her friend about last week's fishing trip.

"Micah held his bag of fish up so proudly. That little one talked non-stop the whole time I prepared the fish dinner."

Susan interjected, "Sounds like you guys enjoyed a delicious meal."

"True. The food was great. While Micah told of his fishing adventures, Jackson bobbed his head in agreement because he could not get a word in edgewise."

"What a great experience for those two. Tell me about this man named Luke."

"God orchestrated that meeting with Luke and his wife Annie. I'm sure of it. I want to tell you the whole story sometime, but for now, I'll say Jackson and I are both impressed with this young couple. Jackson described Luke as considerate and caring. My husband also said how much fun Micah had with him. They evidently bonded in some unusual ways."

Emma settled herself back into the sofa. Susan's right eyebrow arched as she watched her friend get quiet. The coffee cup clinked as Emma absently placed it back on the delicate saucer. She rested back onto the green striped cushion again. Her mind catalogued some of the events of the past couple weeks. As she saw them flash onto a larger-than-life screen, she realized God's hand was diligently at work on her behalf.

She looked up at Susan, "It's amazing how something could feel so overwhelming in one moment and only an hour later feel so different. I did notice how excited Micah was after the fishing trip. What I failed to see was what an incredible breakthrough that whole experience was for him."

"How so?"

"Well, Jackson and I have discussed how reclusive Micah has been ever since the accident."

Susan chimed in, "Rightfully so!"

"Of course. He suffered such a shock and so much loss. But Jackson and I have been praying and hoping to see a sparkle in his young eyes again, and more than that, to see him begin to allow other people into his life."

"Emma, strangely enough it sounds like this young man Luke made quite an impression on your Micah."

"Yeah, I think so, too."

Dinner with the Rhineharts

Emma and Jackson Rhinehart were happy to host Luke and Annie for tonight's dinner. The successful fishing trip from two weeks ago was a hot topic. Jackson told his guests how Emma prepared an out-of-this-world fish dinner that infamous evening. Micah added, "My Lita's a good cook."

Luke asked, "Will there be any Twizzlers for our drinks at the table tonight?"

Micah smiled and scolded, "No, Luke, no loud burping at the table."

"Okay, then we'll see if we can schedule another fishing trip soon."

"Great. I can get the worms when we go."

"That's a deal."

The hosts went to finish some preparations for dinner. Luke's stomach rumbled loudly from the tantalizing smells coming from the kitchen. Annie cast him a disapproving glance. She leaned over and whispered, "I don't think I ever heard your stomach calling out for one of **my** meals." He shrugged innocently.

Annie ran her fingers along the mantle with its prolific display of photos of dozens of children. The infant child in the arms of a young couple could only be Micah and his parents. That squeamish feeling struck Annie in her stomach like it did on the day of the fishing trip when she wondered about Micah's mom and dad.

There was one photo of a little white child standing in the middle of a few dark-skinned children. It looked like they were playing a game with the toddler. Micah said, "They are my hermanos." Annie understood the Spanish word for brothers. She stared intently at the photo and noticed a sparkle in the boy's eyes that was no longer visible in the child who stood beside her. Jackson interrupted with the announcement that everyone should sit for dinner.

* * * *

Luke shook his head and patted his belly. "Wow, Emma, I thoroughly enjoyed that meal, especially the rosemary potatoes."

"Dear, I'm glad to cook for more than just the three of us."

Annie added, "If you're willing to teach me, I'd love to learn to cook like that!"

Pops chimed in, "Emma is a great cook. She has a great dessert lined up, too. For now, let's retire to the living room for a coffee before dessert."

Jackson excused himself to go check on his grandson to make sure Micah was playing close to the back porch. Luke had noticed how quiet Micah was when Annie was there. He wondered if maybe he needed more time to get comfortable with her and vice versa.

Emma said to the younger woman, "I noticed earlier, you were enjoying the pictures of our family."

She admitted, "You sure do have a lot of photos. Is this little baby Micah?"

Emma reached for the silver frame that had the word 'Love' embossed on it, while Jackson entered the cozy living room with a fresh pot of coffee.

He directed, "Please, have a seat. I get the feeling my wife is gonna tell a very tender story."

Luke and Annie were a captive audience as Emma began the story of Micah's mom and dad.

"Micah is our treasure! He is the only son of our daughter Rebecca. She and her husband Timothy had hearts of gold. They spent a lot of time ministering to orphans and young families in Colombia. After Micah was born, they took a couple trips every year. Our daughter, Tim, and Micah stayed in the same two villages each time they visited. Those people became their second family. You could say Micah has lots of siblings. When their little family would come home from trips, Micah would pretend he was still in the village with the kids. He would play for hours in our back yard. He would hide under the bushes and dig to find stones and line them up along the fence. He would tell his parents in Spanish that he was getting ready to play with the children. Apparently, the children did not have toys, so they played with rocks, sticks, twigs, and leaves.

Luke said, "Colombia, huh?"

Annie noticed Luke give her a stare and she understood the unspoken words, *See, that green stone probably is from Colombia. And, it's not yours!* Without a word, Annie's rebuttal in her mind was, *Possession is nine tenths of the law.* Unfortunately, the phrase sounded like a lame excuse for trying to cash in on a gem she did not need. She knew nothing about the stone's sentimental value to this child or his grandparents.

Annie focused on Emma as the story continued, "I remember one story in particular. Rebecca told us the boys would strip some bark from trees and tie the stones together to make dolls. The girls would mix water with the clay and paint the dolls. My daughter noticed that the children had quite a collection. She overheard the kids telling some of the Bible stories they had learned. At one point, the kids told the story about the man dying on the cross and how the rock was rolled from His grave. Rebecca knew that she and the team of missionaries had not covered the resurrection story yet. She was puzzled.

When the kids were telling Rebecca how they knew the story, she just shook her head and cried. The kids told how they all knew of the man with the white light. He was in their dreams. One of the little girls had a dream of Rebecca before she ever came to their village. In the dream the 'white light man' told her a pretty lady with long golden hair would come and teach them more about Him. She would come to the village with a man and a small boy.

Jackson listened to Emma as if he had never heard the story before. He smiled, nodded, and said, "God has comforted us greatly at the tremendous loss of our Rebecca and Timothy. He has helped us to be attentive grandparents. We pray that we will have enough energy to keep up with Micah during his teenage years. But we know how God always provides for us. He's a good Father."

Annie listened raptly and thought Jackson's faith was tangible. This couple has something special with God that she wouldn't mind having. Maybe that kind of faith comes with growing older.

Micah came bursting through the door with a jar full of fireflies. Luke jumped at the chance to play with the little boy. The girls enjoyed their boyish antics.

* * * *

Luke and Annie knew when the time was right, they would learn more about this family. For now, they savored home-made blueberry pie. Emma apologized that the berries were not from their garden. Annie replied, "This pie is off the charts, even if you didn't **grow** the berries." They all chuckled as the hostess shrugged her shoulders.

It was getting late for Micah, so Luke and Annie said their good-byes. The child said "Bye-bye, amigo" to Luke when they shook hands. He gave Annie a little wave as he stepped back shyly. She was okay with that little gesture.

It was good enough for her to see the interaction between her husband and that little boy. Luke seemed younger and energized when Micah was around him.

The young couple was quiet on the ride home. Annie broke the silence with a sniffle, "I thought it was weird that Micah's parents were not around. Now we know Emma and Jackson are raising him and his parents are never coming back. It breaks my heart."

Then Annie burst into a torrent of tears and sobbed for the remainder of the ride.

Micah's Confession

The twenty-minute bike ride to the outdoor farmers' market was so invigorating. The cherry trees were beginning to burst with white and pink blossoms. Annie inhaled the beauty of the day. Her basket would quickly be filled with local veggies and home-made sweets.

There had been an increase in vendors over the past few years. She wondered if that lady with the unique hand-made jewelry would have a booth this season. Annie was rehearsing the alphabet trying to remember the lady's first name, hoping it would dawn on her before she got to the booth. She would be sure to find out if there were any items made with jade.

Annie parked her bike in the rack, looped the mesh basket on her arm, and began her trek through the booths when she ran into her niece Liz and a couple of her friends. Annie smiled as she noticed the girls giggling and looking at a few teenage boys at the end of the aisle of vendors. She said, "Hey, Liz, it's a great day to check out the crafts."

Liz tore her eyes off one of the boys and said, "Yeah, nice day." When Annie smirked, Liz noticed the twinkle in her aunt's eyes. She hugged her aunt and said giddily, "I'll catch up with you later. We need to check out those crafters."

"Yeah, that tall one in the blue shirt and baseball cap looks interesting." Liz winked as she left with the girls.

Annie's favorite things about the market were the delicious smells. She felt like one of those cartoon characters who floats three feet above the pavement being carried away by wafting aromas. She planted her feet on the ground in front of the table of zucchini nut breads. Reaching for a small sample, she hesitated, “I’ll be right back. If I’m gonna taste this, it should be with a fresh java.”

The lady agreed, “Okay, we’ll be right here.”

Annie floated to the vendor three stalls away from the zucchini lady. She ordered a medium coffee when the lady asked, “Have you tried our cinnamon mocha?”

“Cinnamon mocha! I’ll take a large, please.” When she took the first sip, she closed her eyes to savor the delicious blend.

The vendor chuckled, “I wish we could capture your expression, you’d make an excellent advertisement for us!”

When she made her way back, the lady held out the tray of neatly cut squares. Annie filled her cheeks, nodded, and held up two fingers to place her order. The baker said, “I smell the cinnamon mocha special. That goes the absolute best with my bread.” Laughing glances were exchanged as Annie dabbed the crumbs from the side of her mouth, loaded her breads in the basket, and walked farther down the aisle to a vacant wooden bench. Laying her packages on the grass, she settled onto brightly painted artwork of birds and butterflies. This was the perfect stop before continuing her stroll.

As she was finishing her sweet treat, she saw Emma and Micah. “Good morning. How are you two doing today?”

“Well how about that? Your name just came up as Micah and I were chatting. I told him with all these fresh eggs and spices, we should invite you and Luke for brunch tomorrow. By any chance would you two be able to join us?”

"Emma, we’re supposed to watch our nephew Andrew in the morning."

She smiled and said, "The more, the merrier."

“In that case we'd love to come. I'll pick up some orange juice. There’s a guy here who sells fresh-squeezed.”

"Oh good, I'm glad you can make it 'cause I want to try this new French toast muffin recipe my friend Susan gave me." Emma added, "O.J. would be perfect. See you at eleven."

"Thanks, Emma. See you tomorrow. You too, Micah."

Micah dipped his head and gave Annie a shy smile.

* * * *

Annie continued to weave her way through the maze of talented artisans. There was an incredible mix of culinary and other hand-crafted items. She approached the jewelry table and saw it adorned with unusual pieces. Standing to the side of the booth she glanced at the business card proudly displayed on the table. *I only made it to 'G' in the alphabet searching for her name. Thank God for business cards.* Kate, the owner, grinned a greeting to Annie and continued describing some jewelry to a potential customer.

Kate's table was draped in black velvet. Christmas lights hanging from the canopy cast an intricate pattern upon the necklaces and the elegant collection of earrings and anklets. The presentation was as original as each piece of art displayed in Kate's tent.

When the designer finished talking with her customers, she turned to Annie, "Well, it's good to see you at the first market day. How was your winter?"

"My winter was fine. I don't like cold weather, but I love the snow. That sounds like an oxymoron."

Kate said, "Nope. I know just how you feel. I love snow, too. Watching it from my den is my favorite way to enjoy it. I set up my tables next to a roaring fire and assemble lots of jewelry."

"I admire your business savvy. Do you have employees to help you make the jewelry?"

"Not usually. But if the business keeps growing, I might have to hire someone part-time. Why? Are you looking to make jewelry?"

Annie was quick to respond, "No way. One thing I know about myself is that I need to stick to what I do well, which is writing."

"Have I read anything you've written?"

"If you can remember stuff you read seven years ago, then you might have come across something I wrote."

A few ladies began milling around Kate's table. Annie stepped back to let them come for a closer look at the jewelry that was so expertly displayed. She said to the ladies, "Kate does extraordinary work. Her pieces are so classy." To Kate she said, "One of these days, maybe we can share some insider secrets about our talents. Your jewelry expertise and my writing skills."

Kate winked, "That sounds nice. You know where to find me."

As she turned to leave, Annie's eyes fell on a small display in the corner of the table. Green gems?! She lingered but did not want to seem overly interested.

* * * *

The small assortment of fresh vegetables, flowers, and breads fit perfectly into the basket on the front of her bike. Annie hopped on and started to pedal home. Her mind drifted back to those few select green items in Kate's tent. She began to entertain the possibility that Kate might be interested in purchasing a beautiful green gem.

*Annie Livingston, you just told Kate you'd stick to what you know. And... what exactly **do** you know about green stones? Uggh! I almost forgot to pick up the O.J. for tomorrow. Come on, Annie, get your head on straight and stop letting yourself travel to the strange land of* *rocks and stones. Give Charlene a quick call when you get home to see if it's okay to bring Andrew to Emma's house for brunch. Get with the program!* She turned her bike around, grabbed the orange juice, and headed home.

* * * *

The Rhinehart's yard was bursting with spring colors on that glorious Sunday morning. Luke's nephew jumped out of the car and headed straight for the rope swing hanging on the tree. Micah came out of the house and inched his way toward the newcomer. Luke shouted introductions but the boys didn't hear a word. Andrew, who was always larger than life, grabbed the swing and was whooping at how high it launched. The younger boy stood back sizing up the intruder who took over his yard. He dashed towards the garage and ducked into the workshop. He came out sprinting toward the side yard clutching a bucket and two small shovels. When he dove into the mound of dirt on the side of the house, he caught Andrew's attention. Dirt flung as Micah dug quickly extracting three worms by the time the new kid jumped off the swing and rushed to see what was happening.

"Wow, that's so cool. Can I help?"

Micah shrugged his shoulder but did not look up at the stranger.

The visitor spotted the second shovel and began digging next to Micah.

When Andrew held a worm up and emptied him into the bucket, Micah hopped up, ran to the swing, and perched on it like a prize winner.

"Hey, I like your yard. You've got a great swing and this cool place where you can dig up worms. You're really fast at finding 'em."

He looked down from his wooden seat and began to drag his feet in the grass to slow down.

When the swing came to a halt, the older boy said, "Maybe you can teach me how to find worms that fast."

He walked back slowly to the mound of dirt and dropped to his knees. Andrew peeked into the bucket and saw two more worms in record time.

Whistling his admiration as he shook his head, "Now **that** is fast!"

Micah cracked a slight smile and Andrew plunged his hands into the dirt next to his new buddy.

Looking at the exchange between the boys, Annie hoped this could be the start of a great new friendship. Her mind started to plot how to spend time with the Rhineharts and discover more about the green stone.

Jackson had finished setting the table when Annie and Luke walked into the living room. She handed over a lovely bouquet of fresh flowers. The tall, white carnations towered over the yellow and rose-colored snapdragons. The dragons looked like they breathed out fiery red flames onto the other flowers in the arrangement. Jackson nodded his approval and asked, "What are these bright red ones called?"

"I'm not too good on most flower names but I **do** know those are called Celosia Red Arrobona."

"Impressive name!"

Annie was glad she picked up the bouquet yesterday at the market even though it was intended for her own table. She followed Luke's suggestion of bringing the flowers to the Rhineharts. She bummed, *at least one of us is not so self-absorbed.*

Luke carried the orange juice into the kitchen and asked if Emma needed any help. She said, "Well, honey, if you could pour some juice for everyone, that'd be great. The glasses are on the edge of the counter."

Luke said, "You sure you wanna use these fancy glasses?"

“Yes, I certainly do. We rarely have company anymore and I want to serve top shelf.”

“Then fine crystal it is.”

“You can place them on that wooden tray. It’ll be easier to carry everything.”

“This tray is amazing! Is it teak?”

“Yes. It is.”

“The design is beautiful.”

“I agree. Our Tim picked it up for us one of the times he was in Colombia. He found a talented artisan who does wonderful carvings.”

She continued, “It’s a fine piece. I decided to use it and not just put it on display. I believe things are better when they are used for their intended purposes.”

“Would you mind if I put a napkin under these glasses? I’m afraid I might spill something on this work of art.”

“If it’ll make you more comfortable, then sure. The napkins are on the buffet table over there.” Luke reached for the napkins with a relieved look.

The boys came barreling into the house and ran up the stairs. Jackson said, "Whoa, boys. I think it's time to wash your hands and get ready for brunch.”

"But, Pops, I want to show Andrew my rock collection."

"Well, young man, you can do that after we eat."

The boys looked at each other and Micah said, "C’mon, I can show ya the bathroom.” Andrew followed on Micah’s heels. Afterwards, they tumbled back into the kitchen like a tag team, pushing and shoving playfully. Emma shook her head and laughed. Jackson traded tender glances with his wife. She silently hoped, *maybe Andrew will be one of the people Micah will allow into his life. He might be an answer to prayer.*

After Jackson prayed a beautiful blessing, Emma brought the muffins to the table. She handed each boy a stainless-steel shaker. She scooped an extra dollop of whipped cream onto each masterpiece and turned to the boys, "Andrew, you have the powdered sugar and, Micah, you have the cinnamon. Please give a little shake onto each serving." The boys eagerly complied.

The French Toast muffins were a hit. They tasted even better than they looked, if that were possible. Andrew's face was smeared with whipped cream. Luke asked him, "Did you like the French toast muffin?" In response, he bobbed his head and mumbled something unintelligible from his cheeks. Laughter filled the room.

Jackson offered to clean up, but Emma and Annie insisted that the men leave the kitchen. Jackson and Luke headed to the back yard to check out the newly planted vegetables. Luke could see that he was as attentive to his garden as he was to the Chevy. Neat rows were marked with wooden pegs. The names of the plants were obviously written in a child's printing. Jackson pointed to an old wooden bench where they could sit and enjoy the morning.

The two boys scrambled up the steps to check out Micah's rock collection. In the kitchen the ladies fell into easy conversation about plants. Emma had noticed how beautiful the flowers were in the bouquet. She asked if Annie enjoyed gardening.

"I enjoy picking and arranging flowers. I like to harvest veggies from the vendors at the market! My cooking needs work but I can make a killer salad."

Emma replied, "Presenting a nice salad is as important as the rest of the meal."

The younger woman grinned appreciatively.

"Annie, I've probably seen you at the market before, but we didn't know each other yet. It's interesting how we met. I must say it's been even more fun getting to know you."

She agreed with a nod.

After helping with the dishes, Annie went upstairs to check on the boys. She stood at the bedroom door and listened to them chatting quietly. The comforter was littered with rocks. Her nephew was picking up a white one and examining it. Micah offered, “I'm gonna get water so you can see that rock float.”

Andrew countered, "No way.” He looked up as his aunt peeking in the door, “Rocks can’t float. Right, Aunt Annie?”

She gave a little shrug, “Let’s see when he comes back.”

Micah ran out of the room to get water. Huge drops splashed onto the floor as he hurried back to the nightstand with the bowl. He used his elbow to slide the cowboy lamp to the edge of the table and laid the dish down. Micah picked up the stone and handed it back to Andrew. "Here, see for yourself."

He placed the white rock in the bowl, “Wow, cool!"

Puzzlement shrouded his face until Micah told him, “It's lava.”

"That’s amazing.” Andrew looked up at his aunt and asked, “Aunt Annie, did **you** know a rock could float?"

When she came closer for a good look at the lava floating in the bowl, a glimmer from the collection caught her eye. Among those rocks spread on the bed was one that looked familiar. It had the same sheen, jaggedness, and color as her stone. She quickly tried to focus on the floating rock and said, “Yeah, cool, it really can float.”

Then she casually asked Micah if she could hold the green rock. He nodded.

She asked, "What kind of rock is this and where did you get it?" Micah got quiet and hung his head sadly.

“Me and mommy found it in duh village. She told me I had to leave it, but I snuck it in my box. I'm sorry.”

“I don't think they’ll miss it,” Annie told him. She asked, “Is it called jade?"

Micah's eyes lit up, "Yes, that's the name my mommy called it. I wanted to give it back to my hermanos the next time we went to Cow-ombia, but..." He ran downstairs and flung himself at his grandmother. He hugged her and said he was sorry he didn't know that keeping a stone would keep mommy and daddy from coming back from Colombia. Emma plopped down on the chair and scooped Micah into her lap. They held one another and cried. Between heart wrenching sobs, she stroked his soft, light brown hair and whispered, "Sweetheart, your mom and dad did not stay in Colombia because of a stone. There was an accident. That's all. Sometimes accidents happen, even horrible ones."

Micah kept his face buried in Emma's chest as Jackson and Luke came in to find out what was happening. Pops had such a sad look on his face when he saw the scene. Watching them crying and holding each other broke his heart. Hearing what they were saying cracked his resolve and he threw his arms around both and said, "Everything is going to be alright."

Micah's sweet little voice choked out, "Do you mean mommy and daddy are comin' back?"

Jackson said "No, I'm sorry. Mommy and daddy are not coming back. But the Lord is going to provide peace for us. It seems like you've been carrying a great load of guilt upon your small shoulders. That guilt does not belong to you. We don't always understand the way God works. The accident was NOT your fault. Not at all! This does not mean we will ever forget your parents. It just means God is going to give us things in our lives to fill our hearts differently than the way Rebecca and Tim did."

Micah squeaked, "I don't want anybody else to fill my heart, only them."

Emma said, "Only they can fill that particular part of your heart, Micah. But God will fill other parts of your heart with such joy, so the part that misses your mom and dad will not be able to hurt quite as much."

"Like when Andrew came over today? He can be my friend and the part of my heart that needs a buddy will not hurt so bad."

The adults all looked at each other and did everything to hold back a new stream of tears. Jackson replied, "Yep, Micah. God will continue to put people in your life who will love you. He will take care of your mom and dad in heaven while He provides the people and things you will need here on earth. And one day, when we go to heaven to be with Jesus, we will be with the people we love."

Micah liked the sound of that and said, "I can keep missing my mom and dad?" Jackson tearfully nodded his head. The child continued, "My mom told the kids in Cow-ombia that our hearts are like treasure chests. When we ask Jesus to live in our heart, He fills us wif His love. I think I'll like having my treasure chest heart filled up." He turned to Andrew, "Do ya wanna check out more rocks?"

Andrew lit up, "Sure, let's go."

Luke found himself saying huskily, "It would be great if adults could fly with faith like that little guy."

Emma suggested they sit outside with some fresh coffee. First, she excused herself. "I'll catch up with you shortly, if you don't mind." The rest of them went to sit out back. Jackson sipped his coffee and set his cup on the table. He looked up gratefully when his Emma entered the room again. She stood by his side and they shared a tender squeeze before she sat down.

"I suppose this is as good a time as any to let you folks know how we lost our Rebecca and Tim."

Rebecca and Tim's Story

After she made sure the boys were out of ear-shot, Emma found a seat on the back porch. Jackson stood and cleared his throat, "Rebecca and Tim were on a quick trip to the villages, so they left five-year-old Micah with us. After they set up the team of missionaries with the building supplies to construct the homes, they would be able to return home to spend more time with their young son. They met up with some of the men from the village at the Port of Buenaventura to receive the shipment. Jorge was Tim's right-hand man and a beloved member of the family. Micah knew him as uncle. Jorge was a great coordinator when the teams would travel from the United States to Colombia. He knew the land, the people, the rules, and regulations. He was an invaluable part of their team."

Emma shifted uneasily. She prompted Pops, "Continue."

"The plan was to have the supplies transported in three trucks. In the past, the teams had successfully built four homes. The additional challenge for this particular trip was the timing. Other trips had occurred during the dry season; this trip was at the tail end of the wet. The trucks would have to snake their way through the mountains which they knew could be tricky if they had more rain. Tim spoke with us that fateful morning. He felt confident the roads would be dry enough to handle the loads. There was no rain in the forecast.

The roads are not like anything we are accustomed to in the United States. There are pot holes and switchbacks all along the mountain highways. It was the deeply rutted, dirt roads in the woods, closer to the villages that concerned Tim. In the past, he had encountered cavernous holes that could swallow a truck.

We prayed with Tim and Rebecca via skype earlier that day. We knew it would take two days to complete the delivery and a day to travel back down the mountains to be within reach of a cell phone tower. If things went well, we expected to hear from them in about three days. When we got a call from the Colombian police after the first day, we knew that things did not go well."

Annie reached for Emma's hand as a sweet consolation.

Jackson looked pained, "We never expected the immenseness of the news we received from the police. The caravan was traveling successfully through the mountains when a very unexpected storm rolled through with a fierce torrent of rain. Prior to the trip the men had taken precautions and secured extra tarps over the load. One of the tarps had flown off the truck and got tangled in a grove of trees on the switchback they had just passed. The trucks stopped and Jorge ran to retrieve the tarp.

Everything is so valuable to them. They treat things with a greater level of respect than most of us do here in the States. As soon as he reached for the tarps he heard an ungodly noise. At first, he thought it was thunder. He knew in his gut that something terrible was happening. He could see the trucks just up the road from him as the side of the mountain slid under them and took all three vehicles down the side of the steep embankment. They not only fell hundreds of feet, but thousands of tons of mud, trees, and rocks secured their deadly fates. Jorge was in shock for weeks. He struggles with the fact that they all died and he lived. He still keeps in touch with us."

Luke said, "I'm sorry for your loss. So many people were affected by that tragedy."

Jackson could only nod his head in agreement.

Emma said she needed to check on the boys. She leaned against the bedroom door to observe two innocent children.

Each boy was kneeling on the floor to get a good look at the rocks on the bed. Micah taught Andrew some of the rocks' names: jade, lava, and magnetite. Andrew liked the magnetite because a pin could stick to it like magic. Emma tiptoed downstairs.

She told the others, "Those boys are enjoying themselves. Apparently, Micah is quite a teacher and Andrew is an attentive student. It's interesting how our God fits us together. Why they seem just like two peas in a pod."

The sound of elephants startled the adults as the boys stomped down the stairs, grabbed some cookies, and slammed the door while they raced toward the swing.

The four adults broke into uproarious laughter.

Jackson said, "It's astounding how two little kids can make so much noise."

Annie embraced Jackson and Emma longer than normal when they said their good-byes. The elder lady took Annie's hand and patted it with sincere appreciation. Luke signaled to his nephew it was time to go. The two boys waved and shouted, "See ya later."

* * * *

In the car, it didn't take Andrew long to ask, "Is it true that Micah's mom and dad are dead?" Luke responded, "Yes."

Andrew stared out the car window, "I thought it was weird when Micah said his last name was Bridger and not Rhinehart. Anyhow, I'm glad we can be friends. Maybe we can get together more, like going on your boat."

Luke agreed and said, "Yep, sounds good to me. You two are good little fishermen. A trip's a great idea."

"OK, sounds good to me."

An Eye-Opening Trip

The soft, turquoise hues of the Mexican sky matched Annie's beautiful blue eyes on this fine morning. Luke ducked under the wide-brimmed straw hat to place another kiss on those sweet lips.

"Luke, I think I'm in heaven."

He drank in Annie's beauty, studying the curves of her delicate facial features. The pool man approached the couple and delivered two early morning Bloody Marys. Raising their glasses decorated with celery sticks, olives, and fresh sprigs of parsley Luke whispered, "Salud."

Tall palm trees dotted the perimeter of the pool area and cast lacey shadows. The resident iguana peeked his head out from behind the coconut tree closest to them. Annie named the prehistoric crawler, Juan. When his legs unfolded to advance each step, he looked like a dinosaur accented with orange scales on his back. Spooked by hotel guests, Juan scurried under the deck next to the bar where he'd wait for another opportunity to get a taste of some fallen chunks of pineapple.

By the fourth day of lolling, reading, and baking in the sun, the couple was ready to take a short tour of a nearby coffee farm. The locals said it was the most beautiful farm in the area. Luke and his wife boarded the clean, air conditioned, fifteen-passenger tour bus. Their guide Carlos agreed to speak English and interject some Spanish for those who were trying to practice their language skills. It was a lively group. They all seemed to enjoy the scenery as they cruised in the comfortable bus. The canopied fields on the mountainside looked like tents shielding the plants from the afternoon sun. They learned of the "shade-grown" coffee growing process which allows the beans to mature slowly and increases the natural sugar.

The tour of the plantation was enlightening, and the coffee was superb. Carlos assured the tourists any of their purchases would be a help to the farmers. Luke and Annie walked away with seven pounds of rich Mexican coffee.

As everyone piled back onto the bus, Carlos asked if anyone liked strawberries. The little group sounded like a choir responding in unison, "Oooh, yeah!" Carlos laughed and did not say anything more even though they badgered him about what he had in mind. As he gestured with a finger to his lips and said, "My lips are stamped."

The group chuckled as Luke said, "You mean they are sealed."

"Oh yes, pard-ner, I mean sealed!"

The bus jostled half-way down the mountain when the driver abruptly pulled to the side of the road. Carlos stood up and swung the door open. There was a rapid-fire exchange of Spanish between the driver, Carlos, and two weathered locals. Both Mexicans had colorful handkerchiefs tied together around their necks and attached to crates hanging at their waists. Bunches of strawberries rested in the wooden carriers. It looked like a painted scene from an old movie when the models would walk up and down at a sports event with a box dangling at their waists calling out, "Cigars, cigarettes, Tiparillos." Carlos held up a baggie of delicious red fruit. The tourists hurried off the bus to buy fresh strawberries.

As the young American waited his turn on the dusty road, he scanned the beauty of the countryside. Although the fields themselves were well watered, the surrounding landscape was extremely dry. There were rows and rows of delightful vegetation including luscious strawberry plants. Cars passed the impromptu market causing dust to billow, settling a new layer of orange powder on the locals and visitors alike. When Luke turned and covered his mouth with his hankie to avoid inhaling some dust, he saw two wide-eyed little ones clad only in shorts and dirty T-shirts watching the transactions.

The kids were standing away from the road in a sandy ditch. One little guy had an old, beat-up tin pail in his hand. His other hand clutched the shirt of the smaller child. Luke waved to the little ones and tried to position himself under a big tree to grab some shade. The children stood unshielded from the blistering sun, waiting.

It was Luke's turn to buy berries. Using his limited Spanish, he asked the farmer if those were his kids? “Sí, dey are my chil-ren, mis tesoros (my treasures). Dey are egg-sel-ant farm workers. Dey pick berries with me in duh fields most days. Dey are small, but dey are a big help.”

Luke purchased two big bags of strawberries and tipped the farmer generously. “Gracias. Muchas gracias, Señor.”

Annie’s eyes lit up when she saw the size of the strawberries. The bus was quiet as the members of the tour were enjoying the sweet treats. She noticed her husband was not eating berries, he was preoccupied gazing out the window.

She tapped his shoulder, “Earth to Luke. Do you feel okay, Hon?"

"What? Oh, me? Sure. I was just thinking."

“What’s on your mind?”

The bus jolted to a sudden stop and the occupants responded with a collective gasp. Carlos bellowed, “A wake-up call. Feeling sleepy after all those strawberries?” Our guide smiled broadly, “There’s no place like home.”

The group chuckled and gathered their bags.

He thundered, “Enjoy the rest of your stay in magnificent Mexico!”

The Livingstons made their way through the ornate lobby back to their room. No longer wearing rose-colored glasses, the architect took in the exotic fountains and plush furnishings. Couches were decorated in luxurious green and orange fabric, accented with posh pillows wearing ribbons and sparkly gems. Tropical plants placed strategically throughout the lobby gave it the appearance of being outside. Fancy bowls filled with slices of succulent pineapple, star fruit, and strawberries were displayed on elegant tables. *Did they purchase them from a poor farmer with two working children?* Mirrored reflections could be seen easily on the highly polished marble floors. Luke's step quickened with a need to escape to his room to sort through the disturbing thoughts settling on him like dust from the mountain road.

Their opulent room magnified the troubling thoughts of the disparity between the wealthy and the poor. He glanced around the room looking for a place to unload the fruit in his hand. Should he set them down on top of the fully stocked refrigerator or just place them in the hand-blown glass bowl? He turned and handed the strawberries to his wife and blurted, "Annie, are we doing all we can in this world? I have a prosperous architectural business. You're smart, a great writer, and business administrator for James's business. But… are we helping other people in the world?" He paced and ran his hand through his hair, "Obviously, I'm doing a lousy job of articulating my thoughts. I sound as jumbled as the twisted ideas in my head."

Annie released a long, sputtery exhale. "I have an idea of what ya mean." She laid the bag on the nightstand. "I'm surprised to hear **you** with scrambled ideas. I coulda sworn I had the market on feeling mixed up lately."

Luke defended himself, "It's not really mixed up. It's more like… reflective."

She countered, "Okay. Mixed up, reflective, or whatever it's called. It definitely needs some sorting."

"I agree." He looked at his wife and added incredulously, "You've been thinking about how we influence the world around us, too?"

She cast a dejected look, "Your thoughts are **way** more noble than my selfish musings!"

He got up and hugged his wife, "Let's start with what's been on your mind first."

Annie began, "I'm gonna say it's been a few weeks of edginess for me, even before James told me he was cutting back on the business hours." She threw a cautious glance, "I know you're not thrilled about the topic of the green gem, but I think it fits into this conversation."

"How?"

"Let's see. My restlessness started before I found it. When I reached for that stupid stone, it kinda set something in motion inside me. Like a search of some kind. I can't put a finger on it. Whatever **it** is, it's not done yet."

He walked over and plopped himself into the chair and draped his legs over the cushioned arm. "Well. Let's see. I have noticed how tense you've been. I thought it was because of your bike accident. But if something is stirring inside you, maybe there's an issue that needs some attention. These kinds of things have a way of working themselves out. I wouldn't lose too much sleep over it."

Annie countered, "I want to talk with Charlie about a few things."

"Not a bad idea. Charlene's a great listener."

"No offense, but I think **she** might be able to help me. Like you said, things like this usually work themselves out. But it can't hurt to run them by my sister." She turned her full attention to her man, "Enough about me. I wanna hear where your head is. Does this idea of yours have anything to do with those little kids on the side of the road?"

"Yes. So, you noticed them?"

"Sure, Luke, they looked so poor."

"They really got to me. Their dad was bragging about them being hard workers. And the whole time he's talking, I kept covering my mouth with my handkerchief to avoid swallowing the dust. Annie, those kids couldn't have been more than five years old. I can't get them out of my mind. Looking behind them, you could see a little tin shack which I'm sure was their home. Afterwards, when we headed back to the hotel, I felt as if the shades were being pulled back from my eyes. We were surrounded by beautiful mountains, trees, and coffee plantations, but all I could see were run-down shanty homes. I can't imagine what it looks like inside their homes. Anyhow, it got me thinking; especially after hearing how Rebecca and Tim were involved in making better living conditions for the people in those Colombian villages. How are **we** contributing to the good of humanity?"

"You mean like missionary work?"

Luke hesitated, "Not exactly. Maybe we can find some organizations who need volunteers or somethin'."

The young woman sighed deeply. "Well, dear, I have to say… Your ponderings are way bigger than the pebbles rolling around in my head. Maybe, just maybe our thoughts are not so different after all."

Luke tilted his head.

His wife answered his perplexed look, "Things are getting stirred up inside both of us. Maybe a green gem and children on a mountain road are similar. They're unusual and they started moving something in our hearts."

Annie sat back in her contemplations before she went on, "You're the one who said when unusual situations show up, it might be an issue that needs attention. But those things take time to unfold."

A quietness settled on the couple even though their notions continued to swirl.

"Sweety, who knows where all this is going. For now, I'm gonna take a shower and a quick nap. Are you gonna sit by the pool or hang here?"

"I'm taking my book to the pool and finding a spot in the shade."

"Okay, I'll catch up with you in an hour."

* * * *

Luke dragged the lounge chair into the shade to join Annie, "If life's problems need to be considered, this is the place to do it. Sun, palm trees, and a beautiful wife. Suddenly, I don't feel so restless. Guess I'm choosing not to be anxious about how all these things are gonna get figured out."

Annie agreed.

"Remember I told you about the dream Charlene had with me as a princess and my dad as a knight?

"Yes. What about it?"

"I have a strange feeling the stone, the dreams, and even seeing those Mexican kids all have something to do with me getting rid of my fears **and** about you wanting to help others."

"Do you mean if we focus on other peoples' struggles, we can forget about ourselves and find ways to help them instead?"

Annie sat up and almost whispered, "Yeah. I don't know how. But yeah."

"Well, that sounds like good stuff."

"Yes, it does."

She tucked her hair behind her ear slowly, "Who knows, maybe I can help someone else who has experienced pain like my siblings and I have."

Her head shot up and she looked at Luke and cried out, "No way! Luke, you don't think that maybe I can somehow be a help for little Micah?"

It was Luke's turn to stifle a little cry. "Wow, Annie. I think you're onto something."

Annie grabbed Luke's arm. "What am I supposed to do with this? How could I possibly help him? This is so strange. Finding that stone, meeting the Rhineharts, the dreams, and now these local children. It couldn't all be a coincidence, could it?"

"Well, sweetheart, I do know you are a compassionate and loving woman. I can see you helping Micah. You don't have to figure it all out today."

Annie shook her head in disbelief. Luke spotted a familiar glint in her eyes. He liked seeing her eyes light up. It was one of the things that drew him to Annie in the first place.

"One of us is making some headway at sorting. Now hopefully, we can figure some stuff out for me too."

Annie smiled, "Hey, Pal, we're a team, remember? If I have a role in Micah's life, you do, too. Besides, this is a way to contribute to humanity. Don't ya think?"

"You might be right. I like that little boy. It'd be easy to be a bigger part of his life. This calls for a celebration." Luke flagged the server and ordered two beers.

They each sat back in the shade of the palm trees. A breeze kicked up and the kids in the pool screeched as a few of the air-filled floats lifted off the water like kites. Luke got up to chase the one closest to him. He reached for the vibrant ring with the fiery red stripes. Catching it, he turned to the two girls who were running towards him. He held it high and asked, "Does this belong to you?"

Jumping up and down the girls screamed with delight, "Thanks, mister."

Luke sauntered back to his seat and Annie feigned, "My hero."

He bowed low with a sweep of his hand. "At your service, ma'am."

Laughing cheerfully, she said, "Those girls loved you. Did ya' see the older one turn around to bat her lashes at you? Luke, this time to sort things out is making me feel lighter. Less troubled."

He leaned down tenderly and kissed Annie's forehead. "I love you, Mrs. Livingston."

"Luke, seeing you with those kids makes me smile. You have such a nice way with little people. I remember how easily Micah warmed up to you. If I keep hangin' around you, maybe some of your skills will rub off on me."

"You don't give yourself enough credit. Micah likes you and Andrew is crazy about you. That's a pretty good track record in my book." He squeezed her hand, "I'm eager to see what shows up for the two of us concerning Micah and whatever else we need to be a part of." They clung to each other and enjoyed the warm, tropical breeze.

Even the color of the sky lit up with a golden outline around the clouds hanging in the Mexican sky.

Sisterly Advice

Annie stood in Charlene's kitchen watching shadows from the weeping willow dance on the dark granite counter. She listened to the coffee maker as it sputtered the last few drops of the rich Mexican brew into the pot. Charlene slid the newly arranged flowers onto the island, stepped back to admire the lovely mix of red and purple, and asked her sister, "Do you think it needs another splash of color?"

"Hmm. How 'bout if I throw in a few of these daisies, the yellow will soften the red of the geraniums?"

Charlene gave her sister the nod to add the newcomers. "Wow, Annie, I never would've considered adding yellow, but you're so right. The whole arrangement blossomed." They both chuckled at her choice of words.

Annie complained as she sat on the stool with a fresh cup of joe, "Charlene, it's been two weeks since we got home from vacation and I'm still suffering from jet lag."

"Your return trip was so rough with those long delays, roller coaster turbulence, and then your bags getting detoured to Florida. Of course, you're still reeling! How long did it take to finally get your luggage?"

"Two days. Glad that happened coming home and not going **to** Mexico. I don't know, maybe I need more of a change than a vacation."

"Oh great. Luke will love to hear that. You need an **extra** vacation."

Annie shot her an accusing look; Charlie was quick to deflect, "Just kiddin'."

"Alright. Enough negative talk, tell me something positive."

Charlie said, “That's easy. I can talk about Micah and Andrew. Those two have been like two peas in a pod ever since they met.”

Annie exclaimed, “Ha! That’s what Emma called them.”

“Well they sure do like hanging out together. Ray took them to Ridge Ave. Park a few times in the past couple weeks. The two boys came home so dirty after swinging, climbing, and digging up worms. They’re planning their next fishing trip with Luke.”

"How sweet. They’re getting to be good friends.” *I really DID want those two kids to be friends. They were good for each other. My previous plots about using their friendship to uncover information about a green stone feels like a lead weight in my stomach.*

Annie looked at Charlene and finished, “Luke and I thought the boys hit it off right away when we had brunch with the Rhineharts. Too bad for the kids Luke won’t be fishing any time soon because he’s in the middle of designing some upscale stores on Discovery Street. Hey, I’m surprised Jackson and Emma let Ray take Micah to the park.”

"Oh, Jackson went with them every time. Ray said he’s a very nice man. Did ya know he owns an old classic Chevy truck!”

Annie said, “You mean the one that Luke mentions with starry eyes? Yeah, I saw it when the guys went fishing. According to my husband, it’s an expression of Jackson’s wild side.”

The girls giggled, then Charlie said, “In all honesty, there are parts of Jackson’s personality that remind me of my Ray. He’s soft spoken and considerate.”

Annie chimed in, “Yeah and a doctor to boot.”

“Yes, he mentioned it to him. I can definitely picture him as a doctor.”

Annie shrugged her shoulders, *I sound an awful lot like my big sister. I said the same thing about Jackson when I found out he was a doctor. The saying about 'great minds think alike' must be true about me and Charlene. Now I wonder how it can possibly apply to motherhood? Maybe being a friend to Micah is a good place to start.*

Charlene went on, "Emma even went to the trouble of packing some snacks and drinks for them when they went to the park. Ray called her a heck of a baker."

"She's almost as good as you, dear Sister."

Charlene smiled at the compliment and said, "It's so interesting how you met them. Was there any more to that story?"

Annie felt like she was sitting under a naked light bulb with a pull-chain swaying over her head, clinking an ominous sound. *This subject of how I met the Rhineharts was very disconcerting. The green gem certainly lost its luster. The once mysterious stone had become a nuisance. I mentally rehearsed the initial encounter with the Rhineharts and squirmed on this kitchen stool. I made the decision to spit out the* ***whole*** *story to my sister. Besides, I could use some sound advice.*

Charlene knew her kid sister well enough to know there was some kind of war raging in her head. She gave Annie time to process whatever was troubling her. Standing up, the younger sister gazed at the flowers that melded into a kaleidoscope of stained-glass colors. She shook her head to shed the heady aroma, as if the flowers were clouding her mind. Annie loosened her white-knuckle grip from the edge of the granite and started slowly, "I don't think I can tell this to many people. Falling off my bike was only the second part of the story. The first part of the story is somewhat embarrassing. I'm even a little reluctant to share it with you, Sis."

Charlie put her hand on her hip and glared at her, "Are you kiddin' me? With all the major secrets I've told you over the years, you better spill it, Annie Livingston."

She said sheepishly, "When you put it that way, it doesn't sound like I have a choice."

"Right, kiddo. As long as you're not implicating yourself in a crime, you had better start talking."

Annie cringed at the word 'implicating' and Charlene grew concerned, "Annie, are you sure you're okay? I can't imagine that you've committed a crime."

"Not exactly."

"Now, I need a drink of water."

"It's not **that** bad. Some issues I need to deal with have been stirred up."

"Issues! This sounds like the conversation we had before you left for Mexico. Is this about **those** issues?"

"Kind of. Let me tell the story, then you can give me your big sisterly advice."

She anxiously replied, "I'm listening."

"Okay, Okay. I saw an odd stone when I was riding on the bike path behind Emma and Jackson's house. This stone was actually in their yard and I got on my knees and reached through the fence to pick it up. It was beautiful even though it was crusted over with some dirt. Anyhow, when I took it home I thought it might be valuable, so I took it to Sam's Jewelers to have it appraised."

Charlie swallowed hard then nodded at her sister to continue.

"The owner did not give me an official appraisal but when he searched some jewelers' website, I heard him mumble the word jade."

Wide-eyed, Charlie grabbed Annie's forearm and gripped it tightly.

Annie added, "Colombian jade! The morning we went to brunch at the Rhinehart's, the boys were checking out how lava floats. In Micah's rock collection, there was a green stone just like mine. When I asked him if it was jade, he said his mom called it the same name. That's when the little guy admitted to taking the stone from the village in Colombia. He thought since he disobeyed his mom, he was somehow at fault for their death. He probably played with stones just like it in Emma's back yard. Lost it. Then I came along. Now you can see why I think it's jade."

It was Annie's turn to wait. Charlene tapped, rapped and circled the pencil on the counter. She looked up, cleared her throat and began, "Annie, I'm so relieved. You scared me!"

Annie started to talk but Charlene's hand gesture was a loud and clear message to **STOP**! She sat back reticently and waited like a child ready to be scolded.

Charlie continued slowly, "Annie, Andrew told us about the part where Micah admitted to taking the stone from the village. This part of your story explains why you've been kinda nervous lately. Let's see if I got this right. You were willing to get on your knees to reach into someone's yard for a pretty rock that did not belong to you."

Annie looked down, "Ouch."

"Wait. Let me finish."

She swallowed the lump in her throat, moved towards the sink, and stared into the back yard. After a few sips of water, she turned her full attention to this sibling who partially raised her as a daughter. Annie braced herself, but she did not expect what escaped from Charlie's mouth.

"Little sister, this story is bigger than you think. You're only seeing some of the puzzle, not the whole picture. I wanna piece three observations together like I would interpret a dream. Then you can help me if I'm wrong."

Annie nodded.

"First, you found a green gem and it brings two kids together and now they're good friends. That sounds like a good outcome for your personal **issues**, as you call them."

Annie had a glazed-over look.

"Secondly, even though you knew the stone was worth something, you didn't sell it.

"I was contemplating on cashing it in."

"Yeah, but you didn't!"

"No, because guilt almost choked me out! How could I do that to Emma and Jackson, especially after Micah was brave enough to confront his fears and confess what he did?" Annie shook her head, "Brave kid. He's something else, don't you think?"

Charlene's eyes filled with tears as she noticed a softening in Annie she had not seen since they were little girls.

"Charlie, it felt so weird to even consider something like that in the first place. What was I thinking? Luke even asked me what was going on in my head?"

"I'm not done yet."

"Oh, sorry."

"Thirdly, don't you find it interesting how you got on your knees to grab for that stone? Sister, this whole incident is like a picture taking shape. On your knees. Reaching for 'The Rock'. When you put all these pieces together, it looks clear to me that you're seeking God."

"Four weeks ago, I would've said you were crazy. You know how to paint a different picture of this whole mess. Are you saying I'm reaching out to find God?"

"Not exactly. It looks to me like God is doing the reaching. He wants you to believe some things about yourself. Like you're a gem. Like, He intends to take care of you. Those kinds of truths."

Bobbing her head, Annie said, "I was looking for something, I just didn't think it had anything to do with God. Do you think this fits in with my bike dream and the green sweater?"

"Honestly, I think it ties in perfectly. You never told me about the stone, but remember green had something to do with learning about yourself and wearing it proudly."

Annie began to resemble a bobble-head doll.

Charlie began again, "I don't think the gem is necessarily meant to be something to wear. It's deeper than that!"

Annie's hands were getting warm from all the wringing during their conversation. Wiping them on her pants, she said, "I need to go home and sort some things out. This puzzle is not quite clear yet. The one thing I **do** know… the jade has to go back to the Rhineharts." She stood up and said, "Charlene, in record time, you took what I saw as a horrible situation and found the good in it. And you're right, it was unlike me to risk getting my navy capris dirty, yet there I was on my knees."

Charlie shoved at her sister playfully, "Seriously? This is an incredible revelation and you worry about your capris!"

She sighed, "You're always telling me to lighten up, remember? Anyhow, Sis, I've got to admit I didn't think about any of those things 'til you pointed 'em out. Now, oh wise one, got any solutions as to how I should approach Emma and Jackson?"

"Honesty's the best policy in my book. Fortunately for you, the Rhineharts are such sweet people. I don't think you meant anything malicious. You got carried away. Confess everything even though you might feel uncomfortable. Tell the truth. Then simply return the stone that belongs to them."

Annie mumbled, "Easy for you to say. This is going to be hard, but I wanna get this whole stone thing behind me. Then it won't haunt me like it's been doing for weeks."

"That's the spirit, Sis."

Annie's Confession

In the corner of her den next to the handsome gray stone fireplace, Annie stared at the five-foot-tall plant with shiny green leaves. Strong. Vibrant. She could hear Aunt Helen's voice telling the ten-year old Annie, "Occasionally, you dust off the leaves, so they can get more sunlight and grow strong." Why in the world after all these years would those words come to mind? Luke entered the room and the dream-like picture evaporated but the message remained.

Shakily Annie turned to her husband, "Luke, I feel so stupid. Why did I ever consider keeping that stone? I feel awkward telling Emma and Jackson my initial plan. Maybe they won't want to continue to be friends."

Luke grabbed her and held her close. "You underestimate the Rhineharts. They are not people who hold grudges or judge others. This is the time to get this whole thing off your mind. Confession is kinda like brushing dust off a table to see it shine again."

She stared and tried to grasp the probability of him using that particular analogy. She found her voice, "I don't want them to know this part of me. I hate how greedy I was in all this mess."

"My sensitive Annie. Let's pray. It might calm you down."

She bowed her head, wiped the back of her hand across her face, and listened as Luke prayed a beautiful prayer.

Afterward, she stood up with a new resolve to visit the Rhineharts.

* * * *

She parked the car in front of Emma's house, breathed another quick prayer, and headed for the front porch. The faded pinks and violets along the walkway were giving way to golds and blues. Each flower shone with its own delightful hue.

She recalled when Micah offered his favorite bouncy ball. *At that time, I was only annoyed. But now when I think of it, his offer was sweet. Maybe this new outlook will help when I talk to Emma and Jackson.*

Upon reaching the porch Annie remembered Emma bandaging her arm after the bike accident. *How could I be so annoyed then? Tonight, if I focus on how nice they are, maybe I can get through this awful chore.*

Before the young woman knocked, Emma swung the screen wide and greeted her warmly. She said, "Jackson will be down in two minutes, he wanted to get Micah settled so we could talk privately. We both felt like you might need some uninterrupted time because you sounded shaky on the phone. We hope all is okay."

Shyly she replied, "I hope everything will be okay, too."

Emma gave a worried look. When Pops came in, he greeted Annie and told her Micah asked if he could come down and say good night before he went to bed.

"Of course."

Micah stepped down the last two steps slowly while clutching a small, stuffed brown bear. Her smile allayed any of the child's fears, so he held out Mr. Cuddles, "He wants to say good night to you."

"Well, good night to you, Mr. Cuddles," Annie responded as she tugged gently on the bear's arm. She looked into young Micah's hazel eyes. The painful anguish of lonely nights after her own dad died surfaced and she swallowed the golf ball in her throat. She was grateful she had her sister and brother during that dark time of her childhood. This boy had grandparents but no siblings. The ache in her heart almost spilled onto her cheeks. Annie silently prayed for the Lord to show her how to be friends with this child and if there was any way to help ease his pain.

Micah backed away waving the bear's other arm, blowing Annie a good-night kiss. Then he ran up the stairs with Mr. Cuddles. Jackson followed to tuck the child into bed and turned to say, "It looks like our grandson is warming up to you."

Emma added, "Ever since the accident he keeps all females at a distance, except me. His teachers have expressed great concern for him."

Coming back down the stairs Jackson said, "We know healing takes time and we keep praying for Micah to let people into his life. It seems you, your husband, and Andrew have been good for our grandson."

The young woman burst into a flood of tears. Emma handed her a tissue and patted her shoulder gently. When the sobs slowed down, she apologized and reached into her pocketbook. She laid the blue velvet bag on the table. Looking at the ornateness of the gold cords, she wished she had used a plain paper sack. The fancy bag screamed the fact that it held something valuable. Regaining her composure, she explained the whole story to them. She finished the narrative and emptied the jade onto the kitchen table. With a ragged deep breath, she sat back quietly and waited for someone to say something. Anything.

Jackson got up, stood behind her, and rested both of his hands upon Annie's shoulders.

I can feel this man's warmth and strength. His comforting touch reminds me of the time Emma nursed my arm. I'm floating right here in their kitchen. Warm, protected, and comforted. I thought I'd feel shame and guilt, but all I feel is love.

Jackson spoke soothingly, "That was an incredibly brave thing you just did. It must have been difficult for you. The Lord already knows how brave, kind, and truthful you are, Annie. He was giving you an opportunity to discover that fact about yourself. You're trustworthy. You're not greedy. You are **VERY** precious to Him."

Annie began to cry again, but this time it was softly and with such a sense of relief. Sometime during the crying, Jackson sat down, and Emma took his place. She knelt next to the young woman and rocked her back and forth. Through blurred vision Annie could see the small rose buds of her blouse. She rested against this special lady's embrace, soaking up Emma's love, mingling with her own tears.

Almost in a whisper, Emma reminded Annie of her worth, just like Jackson had done. Hearing those words triggered the memory of the green sweater in her dream.

What was it Charlene said when she interpreted the dream? Awakened. To discover some valuable part of my character.

She shook her head in disbelief. *Could all this be happening to show me how loved I am? God used a green stone and a dream to get my attention. It was not to find the value in the stone, it was to discover my own worth!*

Glancing up, she silently prayed, "Lord, you went to great lengths to assure me of Your love and to let me know how special I am to you."

* * * *

Luke heard the car when Annie came home. He stood at the door and noticed how tired his wife looked as she walked up the front path. She snuggled into his embrace when she stepped onto the porch. Luke was not sure whether he was to console or congratulate her.

"I'm okay. Things went smoother than I deserved. The Rhineharts are compassionate people."

"Annie, all talk of cashing in on a stone is behind us. It was a little unnerving. I don't remember ever seeing you struggle like that before."

"Hon, I had to learn some things about myself. It didn't have anything to do with a stone. It had to do with learning how special I am to God. It's hard to explain, but I feel like the whole gem episode was kinda preparing me to help Micah. I don't know **exactly** how. Now, I have some confidence to share some of my life story with him. He doesn't know we have a lot in common. Luke, I want to remind you what I said in Mexico about us being a team. This journey with Micah is not just mine, it's ours. I want to tell you one more amazing thing?"

Luke held her away from his chest and looked dubious. "Really? You want to tell me another **amazing** thing?"

She giggled. "Sorry, babe. This is not 'scary' amazing. It's about Micah."

"Well in that case, go ahead. Tell me." He still looked unsure.

"He blew me a good night kiss. Well, his bear blew the kiss."

"That is awesome!"

"Yeah, I thought so. Anybody else would probably think we're nuts, I mean everybody except Emma and Jackson. They were as stunned as I was when they saw Mr. Cuddles toss me a kiss."

Luke hugged his wife, "This is the beginning of a good friendship between you and Micah. I can feel it. I, for one, am not surprised at all."

She shrugged, "Thanks for giving me all the space I needed to piece these things together. I want to share the other details about my visit, but honestly, I need to rest and take it all in. I love you, Luke."

The Announcement

Two days after the confession, Luke was so relieved to see the beautiful sparkle back in Annie's eyes. *What was it Jackson said? Oh yeah, "The Lord sometimes orchestrates meetings for His own good purposes."* It seems my Annie needed to meet the Rhineharts to get an extra reminder of how precious she is to God... and me. Today is going to be a great day!

* * * *

Luke was still in a great mood when he returned home from work. He lifted his wife up into his arms and kissed her. This time she wriggled out of his arms excusing herself with an air of importance, "Luke, I'm busy with dinner."

He cocked his head, sniffed, and sniffed again. He looked at her and asked, "Did you order from Valentino's?"

"Ha-ha very funny. You better watch what you say to the cook. She might not let you eat this gourmet meal." She turned to tend to the dinner.

"It smells like Emma's cooking."

"She's the one that said something that helped me."

"OK, sounds good. What did she say?"

"It's a surprise."

"Alright, I'm gonna hit the shower. I'll be down in a few. I think I'm gonna like this surprise."

"Perfect, go make yourself handsome." She felt like a new bride serving her first home-cooked meal. She wanted this night to be perfect.

* * * *

He looked yummy in his gray T-shirt when he came down the steps. This time, she was the one who hugged him and nestled her face into his neck. Drinking in his smell, she lingered for a few deep breaths.

He said, “Well, what more could a man ask for? A beautiful wife and the smell of a home-cooked meal.”

She gave him a big squeeze before serving dinner. She thoroughly enjoyed the cries of ‘oohs’ and ‘aahs’ as he enjoyed the meal. “Annie, you did great. This is one of the best meals I’ve ever eaten.”

“Can a trumped-up salad really be considered a meal?”

“It’s absolutely delicious, I’m not kiddin’. What made you think of adding strawberries and grilled chicken?”

“When I was talking with Emma, she mentioned the importance of presenting a nice salad. I took that basic idea and added some fruit to dress it up.”

“And the chicken?”

“Well a cook doesn’t reveal all her secrets but since it’s you, I’ll let you in on it.”

Luke winked and looked around, held up three fingers boy scout style and crossed his heart. “Promise I won’t tell a soul.”

“I bought chicken breast, sliced it, and seared it on the grilling pan to make it look char-grilled.”

He smiled, “Ingenious!” He lifted his glass of wine, “To my wife, the clever cook.”

She lifted her sparkling cider and grinned her deepest appreciation to Luke who was her biggest cheerleader.

“Well, I’m all for your new efforts. I’ll gladly be your taste tester for any future meals.”

Annie thought, *Now, is the perfect time while he's savoring the taste of a good meal.* She started, "Ummm, I've been wanting to ask you a question."

"Hmm, last time you started a conversation like that was when we were in Mexico. Which, by the way, I don't know if we ever reached a conclusion in that discussion about whether we want to have kids. Anyhow, what's on your mind, sweetheart?"

As she handed him a cold drink, she paid close attention to the little droplets of water sliding down the side of the glass. This evening so far felt like a slow-motion night. Annie asked, "You know how I don't like the long, cold winters? By the time March comes I feel like a frozen popsicle."

He responded slowly, "Okay, where's this going? Are you trying to get another trip to Mexico outta me?"

"No, I was thinking maybe in January and February we could spend some time redoing the guestroom. Maybe we can get new carpet, brighten the walls, add a ceiling fan, and update the furniture."

"OK, that might be a nice way to occupy us this winter, but I kinda like the Mexico idea. Warm weather, palm trees, sitting by that crystal-clear pool sipping margaritas with my gorgeous wife."

"That was a great trip. This winter I wondered if we could mix it up. I'll get the magazines, if you wanna look at them before dessert."

"Dessert! Are you kidding? You even made dessert?"

"Only the best for my man."

He patted his stomach, "I can fit some dessert, but it'll have to wait a little while."

"Perfect. We can chat and check things out while the coffee's brewing." Annie glanced over her shoulder with a slight flutter in her belly when she left the room.

When she returned, he exclaimed, "Wow, that's an armful of evening reading! Ever since your break from work, it seems like you've been on some kinda mission."

She ignored his comment and handed him a small stack. Her finger rested on the fan with the ornately carved paddles and tulip-shaped light fixtures." Bouncing her finger on the picture, "I like this one."

"Nice choice. It's unusual." Looking at some of the paint chips, he added, "Wall color and carpet are up to you because we both know whatever I pick, you'll override anyway."

She smirked. "So here are some furniture ideas, tell me what ya think?"

Luke had a puzzled look on his face by the time he leafed through the third brochure. He was shaking his head and saying, "Okay, there's a definite theme here. Is all this baby furniture your way of saying you're ready to talk about having kids?"

She jumped up and said, "We never continued our conversation like we said we would. We were supposed to discuss some serious life changes after Mexico. Remember?"

He said defensively, "We kinda got right back into a life-as-usual routine. We never came to **any** final decisions about ANYTHING?"

Annie looked down and didn't say a word as she fumbled with the edges of one of the brochures absently bending it over and over creating a jumble of the page.

He resumed, "Well, we have time right now. Do you wanna talk about having kids?

Through teary eyes, she whispered huskily, "No, Daddy. I'm saying I'm already pregnant."

He blinked to wade through the clouds of confusion that threatened to choke him. Barely above a whisper he said, "Whaaaat?"

Her head bobbed slowly, "I think you heard me."

He could see flash cards with big block letters spelling the word D-A-D-D-Y. His cheeks grew hot as he blubbered, "You mean we're having a baby? Our own baby?"

"Yep."

Picking up his wife, he swung her around, "I'm gonna be a daddy!" Then he stopped and placed Annie down as gently as a China doll. "Sorry."

She said "It's okay, honey. I won't break."

"We never sat down and talked again after Mexico." He looked down at her belly and tenderly laid his hand on her, "I didn't know I wanted a baby so much. How are you with this whole idea?"

"Actually, I'm thrilled."

"Really, sweetheart? 'Cause I thought you weren't sure."

"Obviously I was already pregnant when I spoke with the Rhineharts, but the stone confession was perfect timing."

"What do ya mean?"

"I **was** searching for something, but it **wasn't** a gem. What I needed was peace about having children. I did not want children in my life because of a paralyzing fear of the possibility of them being alone if sickness or death took me. Those nightmares were crippling. I've been going through a process of letting go of fear and trusting God.

That is what the green stone taught me. When **it** found me, I learned how God provided Emma and Jackson for Micah in his deepest need. I even remembered how my Aunt Helen took care of Scott, Charlene, and me in our time of desperation. Obviously, if tragedy strikes a child, God cares and provides help.

I'm finally ready to trust God. I want to enjoy the blessing of a child in our lives. **That's** what I mean about 'perfect timing'. I'm not afraid. God loves me, you, and all our future children. I trust Him."

Luke stared at her through a fog in his head, he finally spoke up, "Children, huh? Plural? You really **are** growing to trust God. This whole thing feels surreal. Tell me exactly when you found out!"

Her gaze lingered on his dark eyelashes and hoped for their child to be blessed with his stunning features. She explained how the early part of the day started. "I went to Doctor Amin today because I wanted her to give me some B-vitamins or something to boost me out of the lingering jet lag."

During my visit she asked, "Any chance you might be pregnant?"

I scowled and scrunched up my face, "Doc, definitely not!"

She said, "Since we've known each other so long, patronize me, let me do a basic urine test."

"Luke, I looked at her and gave her a dismissive shrug, as if to say, 'You're the doctor.' I remembered thinking to myself, go ahead do the urine test if you want. Then, you can prescribe some major doses of B-12.

When she came back from the lab a few minutes later, she waved the results like an oriental fan and handed them over with a smug look on her face. She congratulated me, and I sat there with my mouth wide open. She sounded like she was at the end of a tunnel when I heard her say, "I wish I could be there when Luke finds out. I have a sneaking suspicion he'll be ecstatic." She instructed her receptionist to set up an appointment with the obstetrician, since I had absolutely NO idea where to start. I think I was in shock. Dr. Amin said the OB will give me an exact due date, but as far as she can tell, the baby's due in late March."

Luke's eyes twinkled, "So, it looks like our winter's not going to be boring. It's my turn to be in shock. Can I do anything for you? Maybe you should sit down and take it easy."

She grinned, "I AM sitting down."

"That's good. Should we hire a maid to do housework for you? Or, or... OK, I sound like a crazy father-to-be!"

"I can't stop smiling. You're making this announcement the best thing in my whole life. Lately, in case you haven't noticed, I've been crying at the drop of a hat. My emotional outbursts make sense now. This explains why I couldn't get over the jet lag." She put her hand on her middle and patted, "**This** is **not** jet lag. This is a real baby." The shudder started in her shoulders and the tears burst like a torrential downpour. Joy flooded her face amidst happy sobs.

Luke held her, shook his head, and let his own tears fall freely. He squeaked out, "Looks like two people who thought they had it all together are falling apart. I have a feeling this is gonna be the norm for the next few weeks or maybe months."

There were more sobs and nervous laughs; then they sat back in each other's arms.

Afterward, Luke got up and poured some coffee and they looked at dozens of pictures of baby furniture. Parents. Imagine that! They wondered if it would be a girl or a boy. Neither of them had a preference.

He jokingly asked, "Hey, what **was** for dessert anyhow?"

"I was too busy preparing a magnificent dinner. I was a little afraid to set my sights too high by attempting to make dessert, so I just bought a carton of ice cream." They laughed and headed upstairs to size up the nursery.

When, they walked into the guest room, Luke saw a stack of magazines on the floor and wondered how Annie managed to amass at least thirty catalogues of baby stuff in such a short time. She flitted like Tinker Bell holding up different pictures from the clippings to demonstrate where each item would be placed in the room. There were at least three entirely different room scenarios. Each plan included pale green walls and furniture. Her imagination included stuffed zebras, camels, giraffes and bears finding their home in the nursery. He began to wonder if there would be enough room for the baby.

He sat on the carpet with his back against the wall. Annie continued her decorating as Luke mentally renovated this into a charming nursery. He incorporated her color scheme into the plan. He'd strike a line thirty inches from the floor all the way around the room and install olive wood panels. They would make a perfect background when their little girl played with her kid-sized table, chairs, and tea set. If it is a boy, he could use the tops of the trim to attach hooks to support his make-pretend forts. 'Daddy' created a unique wall with protruding bricks for a castle parapet where kids could play and hide. When he constructed the wall, he was transported to his childhood yard with his brother Paul who was thirteen years older than him. They spent hours together in faraway lands in caves, ships, and deserted islands riddled with hide-outs, gang-planks, and other traps skillfully hidden from their enemies. The bad guys never had a chance against Paul and Luke, the unstoppable duo.

He hoped this fantastic news of a new baby would entice Paul to leave his beloved Spain to visit Luke and Annie and their child. His brother had not been to the United Stated for many years. A sadness blanketed Luke during this celebration. He longed to see his only sibling and his two nephews, Jacob and Brian. This father-to-be was not only dreaming up plans for a beautiful nursery but for a family reunion as well.

Annie's voice snapped Luke back to the present. Between his expertise in architecture and his wife's creative flare, this room will look like it could be featured in a magazine. They decided to hold this **baby** secret to themselves until after Annie's visit to the obstetrician.

The news would be hard to contain since both would be walking around with permanent grins on their faces.

News from Far Away

The following week when Luke heard that Ray, Andrew, Jackson, and Micah were going to play ball, he asked if he could join them. Ray said, "Of course, meet us at the Ridge Avenue fields."

"OK, I'll look for you guys in an hour."

The boys couldn't tumble out of the car fast enough at the park. They both raced across the grass, touched the fence, and raced back as if there was a pre-planned field event. Luke was getting out of the car when the boys spotted him. Andrew yelled, "Hey, Uncle Luke, did you bring your special baseball?"

Luke held it up, "Yep, it's right here." He tossed him the light weight, over-sized ball. Andrew turned and tossed it to Micah. He caught it and stared at the ball resting in his hand. Elated, he yelled, "Pops, I really can catch this ball." Grinning, they positioned themselves to have a little fun.

It was a comedy of errors as the men took turns pitching and the boys took turns missing. The men changed strategies and practiced throwing the ball to each other. The little guys preferred the swings and monkey bars. They were tired of attempting to hit a baseball. The men talked while the boys exhausted themselves on the playground.

Jackson told them how Jorge recently called to tell of the struggles the families in the Colombian villages were having. Apparently, a water source had run completely dry. Some of the elders were considering relocating their village on the mountain. Both Luke and Ray were concerned for this group of people they had never met. Ray was the first to shoot a question to Jackson, "What was their water source before it dried up?"

He described the shallow well which was supported by leftover lumber from the homes Rebecca and Tim constructed two years ago. A church group from Minnesota donated a drilling apparatus to the village. The missionaries collaborated with the locals to build the well. A different group from Florida provided a purification solution to assure the water was potable. Those Floridians had proven to be faithful supporters ever since.

Luke said, “Wow, they sound like generous people.”

Jackson continued. “Supposedly, the quality of the water is not the issue. The actual ability to draw water from the well is the problem.”

Ray asked, “How are they handling it?”

“Jorge is a clever man with a heart of gold. He negotiated with a nearby village to use some water from their well. You must understand, it’s not like going to the next town here in the States. These villages are not very far from each other, but they’re separated by some rough terrain. Jorge has been in touch with the Minnesota missionary group to inform them of the plight. A mission team is expected in fifteen weeks, so they can assess the situation. In the meantime, they’ll have to visit their neighbors’ well.”

Andrew and Micah interrupted the conversation to tell the men they were hungry. Luke took his backpack, opened it, and handed the boys a couple apples. They ran back to the bench at the playground shouting their thanks. Ray said, “Hey Luke, for not having kids you sure are prepared.” Luke had a twinkle in his eye but remained quiet.

Luke suggested sitting down in the shade as Jackson continued his story. The retired doctor said, “There’s not much else to tell. The situation is grave, they need to rely on the Lord, we are too far away to help other than with prayer.”

Ray wondered aloud, "Surely things can be expedited quicker than fifteen weeks."

"Honestly, I think Jorge is doing all he can at this moment."

"What if there were other resources available?"

Jackson looked at Ray, "Such as…?"

"You know I work for The Water Company. Did you know I'm a research analyst?"

"No, I didn't."

Ray continued, "In addition to designing water systems for local areas, we conduct research to establish viable water opportunities for remote villages, globally. I was not aware the villages in the mountains of Colombia had a water problem."

Jackson timidly inquired, "Do you think the Water Company could help?"

"We sure can find out. First, I think it's a good idea if we adults could meet without kids, so we can have an uninterrupted discussion about Jorge's situation." As if on cue, Jackson got hit on the side of the head with the kid-friendly baseball, which was not very adult-friendly.

He rubbed his head saying, "No interruptions sounds good to me."

Luke offered his home. "Let's meet tomorrow night at my house. I already have some ideas brewing."

Jackson cleared his throat and added, "I would like to include the ladies and it would be wise for us to invite the Lord to our brainstorming session. We certainly want to follow His lead."

All three men agreed.

Ray offered, "My daughter Liz would be more than happy to keep an eye on Micah. Can you drop him at our house tomorrow around seven?"

"OK, it's a date."

* * * *

Ray gave his daughter a hug, "Thanks, Liz, for watching your brother and Micah on such short notice."

Liz pulled her thick wavy hair back into a ponytail, "No worries, Dad. I'm looking forward to meeting the Rhineharts. Uncle Luke says Micah's a neat little guy. Besides, I finished the project I was working on for our writers' group, so I'm free."

"You finished it already? Wow. I'd like to read it."

"Okay, maybe later, I want to run it by Aunt Annie first, then I can show you the polished piece."

Ray respected his daughter's wishes and withheld the teasing remark he almost made. Instead he replied, "Great idea. Annie is the expert when it comes to writing."

When the bell rang, Andrew flew down the steps and flung the door open. It thudded as it slammed the wall and Charlene came out of the powder room exclaiming, "Andrew, is all that commotion necessary?"

He turned and looked at her, "Mom, Micah's here."

Charlie smiled, "I can see that. I'll be out in a few minutes."

Ray came to the rescue to properly welcome Emma, Jackson, and their grandson, "Please, come in."

Jackson held onto Micah's shoulder as he extended his other hand to the host, "Hi, Ray."

Stepping aside, "You know our exuberant son Andrew, and this is our daughter Liz."

Emma and Jackson replied in tandem, "Nice to meet you, young lady."

Micah remembered Pop's instructions and timidly extended his little hand to her, "Hello. I'm Micah."

She crouched to his eye level and shook his hand, "Nice to meet you, Micah, I'm Liz."

"Yeah, Andrew told me he had a sister."

Andrew locked arms with his buddy but before they scrambled off, he looked over at Ray, "Dad, can I show Micah my new rock?" Ray gave a nod and Micah glanced up at his Pops to get a nod from him too. The boys fled to the den. Andrew dumped the few rocks from the soft, leather pouch onto the square velvet mat on the table.

Emma said, "Well, that went better than I could have imagined. Those two seem to be fast friends and Micah's quite comfortable with you, Liz."

"Yep, looks like we'll be just fine."

Charlene joined the group and welcomed the guests. "It looks like we're gonna have some adult time tonight."

Emma glanced into the den and asked, "Do you mind if we say a good-bye?"

"Not at all. follow me." Charlene walked slowly, yet gracefully, with the support of her crutches. Liz followed them into the den and found the boys deeply engrossed examining rocks in both collections. Emma hugged Micah's shoulder, "Pops and I will only be a few minutes away at Luke and Annie's house. If you need us for anything, just ask Liz. Micah nodded but was staring at the shiny magnetite. Jackson shrugged his shoulders and led Emma quietly out of the room. She looked a little dismayed. When the four adults headed for the door to leave, Micah came running into the room, hugged Emma and told her, "I'll be okay. Have fun, Lita." He ran back into the den.

The older couple got in the back of the black Suburban. They watched Ray maneuver the four-pronged foot stool close to the car for Charlene to get into the vehicle. He gently steadied her and made sure she was comfortable; then handed her the crutch that was her trusted companion. Jackson made a move to help but thought it best to let Ray handle his familiar routine.

After they drove for a few minutes, Emma sniffled and blew her nose as she said, "That grandson of mine is such a sweetheart. He acts so brave but he's still a little boy with all kinds of uncertainties running through his head."

Charlie also had moist eyes, "I can see what you mean about him. He is a sweetie."

The grandmother continued, "I'm sure your Liz will take good care of him. He seemed to like her right away. She has a way with kids, huh?"

Ray piped in, "That's our Liz. She's a good girl. I have to correct myself, she's a fine, young lady." At that, Charlie smiled at Ray and reached for his hand across the middle of their seat.

Charlene spoke up again, "Emma and Jackson, do you think these discussions tonight will be difficult as you remember all the work Rebecca and Tim did in Colombia? Will it be too painful for the both of you? I don't want to see you guys suffer any more."

Jackson answered, "Sometimes, even though there is a level of pain involved in a season of life, there is a greater joy that outweighs the pain. Emma and I prayed a lot last night and we're ready for this evening. We want to be involved in helping the people our daughter and Tim regarded as their second family. We're honored to be a help and we're looking forward to working with all of you." Emma wiped her nose for the second time tonight and looked at her husband with such gratefulness. Charlene glanced in the visor mirror to see the tender exchange between the two of them. She leaned to the side of her seat, reached around toward Emma and discreetly handed her another tissue.

As they pulled into the driveway, Ray quipped, "We're here. Let's get this adventure started."

The yellow daffodil faces smiled at them and the low-lying waxy begonias lined the path like a red carpet. Two lanterns cast a warm amber light onto the brick patio. The doorbell chime announced their arrival. Luke threw open the huge, oak door. The entryway was aglow with flickering candlelight. Two planters containing large silk hydrangeas graced each side of the entryway. An old-fashioned watering can was suspended in mid-air above one of the plants which created a whimsical touch. The host welcomed them with a grand, sweeping gesture, "Good to see you guys… and girls."

Charlene laughed, "Such chivalry, Luke."

"Okay, get in here. How 'bout a big hug for my favorite sister-in-law?"

"What about your other sister-in-law, Karen?"

"Lemme give you a hug, Charlene." They embraced, and he gave an extra squeeze for good measure.

Jackson and Emma smiled at the ease of the loving banter. The others greeted each other warmly. Emma commented, "I love your home. I assume you designed it, right Luke?"

"Thanks. Yes, Annie and I designed it together."

Annie leaned into the room from the kitchen, "Did I hear my name?"

"Yes, the gang's all here. Let's get settled in the den."

She waved her hellos and said she would join them shortly. Charlene offered to help, but the reply was, "No thanks, I kept it simple. For now, I'll bring us a tray of some waters."

"That works for us," Ray replied.

As they were getting settled in the den, Annie entered with a tray of glasses and a pitcher of water. She placed the tray down on the large, dark wood coffee table and greeted her guests properly. After all the hugs and hellos, she began to pour some waters and burst into tears. Immediately, Luke jumped up next to her, "Sweetheart, are you okay?"

She quieted down, "It's ironic how I could so easily offer a glass of water when the Colombians dig for it, carry heavy pails of it, and work so hard to get it. We have so much to be thankful for."

Luke agreed, "Let's get right down to business." He sat close to Annie on the loveseat and continued to hold her hand.

Jackson spoke up, "I believe we know the first order of business." He took the initiative to begin praying. They each added personal, heartfelt prayers. There was a genuine outpouring of love and an awareness of being loved by God. An incredible electricity permeated the room. It was almost tangible. Then a silent hush and an awesome sense of peace rested on this newly formed team. It set the stage for the brainstorming and the all-important discussion to follow.

* * * *

Next, Ray took the floor, "Several years ago, The Water Company developed a portable set of pipes affectionately known as the 'pipeline'. There's a unique drill bit which is attached to the head of the pipes. The Water Company researchers knew they would be operating in places where electricity would not be accessible, so a battery-operated motor was designed to power it. Of course, we can't reach as deep as our hydraulic rig but it's portability is ingenious!

The drill bit is designed like a medical intravenous needle. The bit penetrates the earth like the needle pierces the skin. In the IV, the needle retracts, leaving the cannula tube under the skin. We call our equipment **AX-S** and when the drill bit is pulled back to the surface, a durable tubing, which is our version of a cannula, creates a wall-type sleeve to hold back the surrounding dirt. Can you picture how our tools replicate an IV?"

All heads nodded, Annie was the only one taking notes. She paused mid-sentence and raised her hand. Ray responded, "Yes, Miss Annie, do you have a question?" The group chuckled. She relaxed and queried, "Do you have any pictures to help us understand the process?"

"Yes. You're slightly ahead of me. I do have some drawings to show you."

Luke added, "Ray, I think you missed your calling. You could've been a teacher."

"I appreciate the compliment, but, class, I'm not done yet. There's more to explain."

This time Emma chimed in, "Okay, Ray, you have the floor again."

Ray took out a drawing of the well, the bit, and the river of water at the bottom. Luke and Annie jumped up to remove the tray and glasses. When all was cleared and the drawing spread out, Ray pointed to the thin cylinder running vertically from the top to the bottom of the drawing.

"This is our **cann.** When it's secured, we cause a mini detonation which enlarges the access to the water, then a pouch of screening material is tossed down the chute and wedged at the bottom."

Luke questioned, "Is there a possibility the explosion could compromise the bottom of the cann?"

"We are confident the explosion will discharge down into the stream rather than up the equipment. The technology employed here is the same principle used in pyrotechnics."

Jackson asked, "You mean fireworks?"

"Yes, sir. I could explain the physics but suffice it to say the research proves the success of directing the explosion."

The chatter among the group began and Ray let them check out the drawings. He was certain that if they could get a clear picture without getting bogged down in scientific details, they would put their wholehearted support behind the project.

When things quieted down, Charlene commented first, "For those of us who have no idea whatsoever about drilling for water, can you slow down a little."

Ray smiled at his wife while his brain was trying to release the hundreds of needles pricking his memory of Charlene's encounters with as many IVs. Testing for Multiple Sclerosis was a marathon of endurance that held an ominous verdict. He recalled her bruised arms and sunken cheeks but the sparkle in her eyes only waned temporarily. Charlene rose like a phoenix after so many tests and trials. Her smile would dispel fears that attempted to unravel the family. MS has been a cruel master but could never be outdone by Charlene's faith. He admired his wife's tenacity.

Ray looked at the love-of-his-life and smiled at her enthusiasm. "Sure. But I thought you'd grasp this concept quicker than most of us here."

"Really? Why?"

"Because you've experienced your fair share of IVs."

Tears welled-up in Annie's eyes as she walked over to squeeze her big sister's shoulder.

Charlene shrugged, "The comparison to an IV is incredible. I just want to get a closer look at the pictures, so I can see what it looks like in the earth rather than in an arm." Ray nodded. They crowded to get a better view of the drawings.

Jackson quietly broke in, "So, Ray, could you explain what happens after the explosion?"

"Sure. After the detonation, a small sack of screening is inserted into the cann. It acts as a filter to catch any large unwanted particles from making their way up the tubing."

"Can the screen filter out bacteria?"

"Here's a copy of the bulletins listing the types of bacteria it is designed to block."

Emma added, "Will the water from the well be tested?"

"Absolutely, but I think once Jackson has read the Bacteria Data Sheet, he'll have a better idea of what solutions to use to assure potable water."

The doctor commented, "It looks like I have some homework to do for this project."

Glancing around the room, Ray added, "Any other questions?"

The group got quiet and Luke responded, "No more questions, for now. Hopefully we can move quickly on this."

Annie winked at her husband and mouthed, "Looks like we're finding another way to help others."

Ray resumed, "As a team, let's decide which tasks each of us wants to handle."

Jackson addressed Annie, "Do you think you could draft a proposal for the Water Company to get the necessary equipment?"

"I already have some good ideas for the letter."

Luke signaled his wife to join him in the hallway. "Hon, does it sound crazy if I plan a trip to Colombia?"

"This chance is being dropped in our laps. If you don't go, it would be like ignoring a sign."

He hugged her and whispered in her ear, "What about you and the baby?"

"Daddy, we'll be fine."

Emma asked Charlene, "Wanna team up with me to contact the groups from Minnesota and Florida and ask if they would like to help?"

Charlie loved the idea of working with Emma, "Sure thing. Maybe Andrew and Micah could play together as we do our part for the cause."

"I was hoping you'd say that."

When the girls finished planning, the guys were already in the kitchen grabbing some coffee. Luke was looking at possible dates to block out of his schedule for a trip to Colombia. If the Water Company granted approvals quickly, a team could be ready in about seven weeks. It would be considerably sooner than the other missionary group could get there. He brought some coffee into the den for the girls. Annie spoke up, "I was wondering if you guys would mind if I put together a calendar showing what each person is handling?"

"What a great idea. That'll help us to see if there is anything we might have overlooked."

"I think we all know my sister is the best candidate for keeping us organized and on task."

Ray concluded, "Well, it looks like we have our work cut out for us. Let's each keep our new secretary in the loop, so she can track our progress. Annie, can you update us via e-mail?"

"Certainly."

Luke added, "Ladies, when the guys were in the kitchen, we agreed that a trip to Colombia is needed in a few short weeks. The date depends on how quickly we can get Water Company approvals. What do you girls think? Can you do without us for a few days?"

There was a unanimous agreement from the girls. Emma said, "This is a huge challenge to see my husband return to the place where we lost Rebecca and Tim." Her eyes met his, "If you think you're up to the task, then I can pray as you go."

"Thanks. I think the harder part will be when I suggest that Micah accompany me."

She looked downcast, but her response was one that defined the courage she embodied. "I thought you'd be taking Micah with you. My prayer group had some prophetic words a few weeks ago about preparing myself for a separation which would result in a great accomplishment. I believe this trip will prove to be successful. Not only will the villagers get water, I think there will be healing for some of us."

Jackson crossed the room and enveloped Emma in his arms. Each man followed suit and stood with their wives. The doctor prayed a quiet prayer to conclude the night.

Ray said, "Annie, we'll be waiting to get your e-mail updates. That should save us lots of phone time." The two younger couples added notes to their cell phones and Jackson wrote the e-mail information on a piece of paper. He assured them, "Emma and I are on board with the whole idea and we'll do our best to become more proficient with the computer to keep in touch."

Ray turned to Luke, "Well buddy, you better practice your Spanish. It looks like we're going to Colombia to dig a well!

PART TWO

* * * *

Arrival in Colombia

Preparations for the Trip

The seven-person team had operated like a well-oiled machine for the past fifty days. All necessary equipment and man power for the 'Colombian AX-S' job was seamlessly put into motion. Annie had written an amazing proposal for the Water Company, and Ray's boss signed the approvals in record time. The women sewed interesting totes which were used to transport the lighter tools. Charlene and Emma were delighted when the groups from Minnesota and Florida offered to maintain the wells once they were drilled. Micah spent time gathering rocks to bring as gifts for the village children. Ray had been busy educating Jackson and Luke about the details of the well-drilling process. They proved to be attentive students.

Large equipment was shipped and scheduled to arrive in the Port of Buenaventura the day before Ray, Jackson, Luke, Micah, and the two engineers would touch down in Colombia. Ray was glad to have the additional expert help from the Water Company as a part of this team.

Before the six Americans left the States, Jorge had called to inform them that the supplies arrived safely. Everything was securely stacked on the trucks. All systems were 'go'. Jorge would pick up the Americans at the airport tomorrow.

On the Flight

Luke greeted the two strangers seated next to him on flight #626 then shifted his body to look out the pane which framed his field of vision. Instead of seeing the airport and ground fall away, he could picture his sweet Annie during those early morning hours sitting hunched on the bathroom floor hugging the toilet. *How could she look so beautiful in that position, with her blonde hair knotted on the top of her head and loose, wispy strands outlining her pale face? Despite all that, when she looked up at me, she shrugged her shoulders with a weak chuckle.*

The most bizarre part of the early morning ritual was the 'gong', which is what he and Annie affectionately called it because when the clock would strike nine every morning, she would stand up from the floor and continue her day as if the bathroom episode never happened. It was as if nine o'clock magically signaled the ritual's end. So far, that routine was the most obvious indicator their family would be expanding.

They both agreed to keep quiet about the baby at least until the men left for Colombia. He remembered when she told him, "Those wheels won't be off the ground, and I'll be running to Charlene's house first, then I'll be calling my brother Scott, and finally Emma. I'm about to burst with this news. Of course, I'll ask them to keep the secret from Ray and Jackson."

He patted her hand at the time and complimented her discipline. He knew the family would celebrate exuberantly with the incredible news. Luke wondered if Charlene might already have an inkling about the pregnancy.

Life had changed in the past seven weeks. He and Annie would plot and plan everything **baby**. Names, nursery decorations, clothes, even where the baby will eventually attend school. They developed a code word if anyone was within earshot of their voices, so they wouldn't spill the beans. It had been fun to have such a precious secret.

Two days ago, Jackson invited Luke for a cup of coffee. Men only. They enjoyed quality time as they recalled some of Andrew and Micah's antics during their fishing trip two weeks ago. Luke learned a lot about parenting when he watched how the retired doctor handled the rambunctious boys on the boat. His visit with Jackson was a much-needed change from work, home, and all the plans for this trip.

Luke arched his back in his cramped seat, put his head-set on, and tried to catch a nap before they touched down in Colombia in less than three-and-a-half hours.

The flight attendant was reaching for his tray table to secure it. She smiled at him and said, "I hope you enjoyed your nap." Startled, he tugged at his ear bud and it dangled like a swaying timepiece against his chest. He looked at his watch, shook it, and held it to his ear. Glancing out the window, the ground quickly approached them, and the towering palm trees came into view. *More than three hours of sleep on a plane? Apparently, I was exhausted!*

Sharing Baby News at Home

Annie wove in and out of traffic after dropping the four men at the airport. A dozen ways were rehearsed to share this news with her sister. Stopping at the florist to pick up a lovely spray of flowers for Aunt Charlene was her final choice. Wrestling the basket out of the passenger seat was comical since the pink and blue balloons kept getting stuck on the seatbelt. When Annie looked up from her contorted position, Charlie was standing on the steps laughing. "What in the world are you doing, Sis?"

"Charlene, go back in the house this instant!"

She saluted her sibling and retreated as ordered.

Annie used her hip and foot to open the door to the house. Success! Balancing the basket, she laid it carefully on the kitchen island. Charlene decided to greet her sister by yelling from the safety of the back porch, "Is it okay to come in?"

"Of course. It's your house."

"Ha-ha. A few minutes ago, you almost bit my head off, remember? I was trying to give you space. What's this all about? Are you celebrating the guys leaving?"

She labored to put her crutch in its usual place, but it hit the floor with a thud. Annie quickly retrieved it. "Are you okay?"

"Yep. Just real curious about what you're up to."

Annie handed her sister a glass of iced tea, "Well, let's raise our glasses in a toast."

"It's customary to know what we're toasting."

"To Aunt Charlene."

Charlene screamed before the conclusion of the rehearsed toast. They fell into each other's arms and cried with delight.

"How long have you known?"

She casually picked at her fingers, "I'm nine weeks."

"Nine weeks? How did you ever keep it a secret?"

"Luke and I didn't want to tell the team because we knew Ray would try to talk him out of the trip."

"Well, you're absolutely right!" Charlene hesitated a moment then added, "I think Luke made the right decision."

"Thanks, Sis. It was hard for the two of us to keep quiet, but now it's gonna be a blast telling the whole world about Baby Livingston!"

"I agree. Wait! Does that mean you were pregnant when we had the first meeting about Colombia?"

"Yes. That's why the sobbing when I tried to serve water."

Charlene threw her head back and laughed 'til she cried again. "I pride myself in being observant, but little sister, I certainly did **not** see this!"

"This is the **best** news. I have lots to fill you in on."

"You sure do." She grabbed Annie's hand and led her to the porch. "Have a seat. I'm gonna get our drinks."

"I can help."

"No, this time let me serve you. Besides, I think I'm too excited to sit right now. Mom and dad would've been thrilled."

Annie refrained from any comment.

Charlene relished every last detail, especially the part about the morning 'gong'. "This baby is going to be so much fun."

"You know, Charlene, ever since I returned the stone to Emma and Jackson, it's been like a boulder was taken off my shoulders. I appreciate you helping me work through that stuff."

"Well, it looks like you got through all that, so you could focus on the baby."

"That's what I told Luke."

After an hour of baby talk, Charlene said, "By the way, it sounds like the guys got off okay. Ray called from the airport before they took off. He'll call again when they land."

"Yeah, Luke too. He is on cloud nine. It took a lot for him to get out of the car and leave today."

"He'll be okay. They have a lot of work in front of them – more than enough to keep his mind occupied."

"Ten days is a long time, I'm gonna miss him desperately."

"I'll miss Ray, too. It's gonna be a big trip for them. By the way, did Emma invite you to her prayer group?"

"Yes. Are you going?"

"Sure. I'm looking forward to it. Wanna go together?"

Annie looked down at her belly, "That's a good idea, all three of us can go. But for now, should we give Scott a call?"

"Absolutely. I think he's gonna be quite surprised."

Emma

Standing up, she gently shifted her weight to release the garden hose kinks settling in the middle of her back. Emma wiped her brow thinking, *I can't do this kind of strenuous work the whole time they're gone. They'll come home to find me hospitalized from fatigue.*

I'll pace my physical activities. Who woulda thought a person could miss two guys so much, and it's only been four hours since they left. Oh Lord, I need an extra measure of peace. Amen.

As Emma pushed a few strands of hair away from her face, she noticed Annie's car glide into the space directly in front of the house. Her throat constricted, hoping all was well.

The balloons bobbed on the cute basket Annie was carrying. When she reached Emma, she held out the basket to her. "Good afternoon, Emma. This is a Nice-to-Meet-You gift."

She wiped her hands on the apron before she accepted the gift, "How lovely." She looked past Annie and bent to look in the car. "Who am I meeting?"

She patted her tummy and beamed, "I'd like you to meet Baby Livingston."

"Annie, this is the nicest surprise. I feel like I'm going to be a grandmother again."

They hugged, and an encore of waterworks began.

The Airport in Colombia

A few weeks ago, Emma, Charlene, and Annie made canvas bags which held five-gallon buckets, lids, and liners. The odd-shaped carriers were a creative solution for carting the unusual contents. Even Micah maneuvered the luggage quite easily with the retractable wheels.

A lady with three sons clumsily toting their own luggage, asked Luke, "Where did you find those bags? They look so easy to handle."

Micah proudly answered, "My Lita made them."

She smiled at the boy, "Well your Lita did a great job!"

The entire team met at the baggage claims area. Micah was excited, nervous, and exhausted. He wanted to ride on a luggage cart and Pops said, "Hop on, I'll steer." The seasoned doctor knew this trip was going to be highly emotional for his grandson. Jackson was sure Micah would get flooded with memories of his mom and dad. For all those reasons, he intended to keep an extra close eye on this beloved child. He was grateful knowing that Emma and her prayer group would be praying for the team while they were here in Colombia. That fact would continue to give Jackson solace and courage to complete this task. He knew this was not just about water. This trip would go deeper than that.

Before they headed out the doors to find Jorge and the two trucks, each man found a quiet spot where they could contact their wives. Jackson and Ray texted their wives to update them about the flights and the nice compliment they got about their 'unique' bags. Luke punched in his wife's number.

Annie picked up on the first ring. "Is everything okay?"

He smiled, "You stole my question. Flights were great. I was thinking so much about you and the baby. How are ya feeling?"

She giggled, "We're fine, but we miss you already."

"I have been gone a few hours and I miss you two so much."

"No worries, Dad. Girls can find ways to keep busy."

"Girls, huh? Do you know something I don't know?"

"Not really. Just call it a hunch."

"Well, boy or girl, take care of each other. According to Jackson, phone reception is tough, so I'll contact you when I can. I love you. Both!"

"We love you, too."

Knowing that all was well at home, the team proceeded to look for Jorge.

Micah grabbed Jackson's hand and said, "Pops, my belly feels funny."

"Micah, is it painful or does it feel kinda twitchy."

"Yeah, Pops, twitchy. Do you think I'm sick?"

"No, I think you're nervous. There are people here that love you and will be glad to see you. You will be alright."

"Pops, I'm gonna hold your hand real tight, ok?"

They clasped hands again and Jackson was not sure if the moisture was from his own hand or from the smaller one. He bent down and hugged some reassurance into Micah.

Stepping outside into the warm Colombian air, the team was greeted with the noise of speeding taxis and the loud clamoring of people. The palm trees swayed in the warm breezes and bright hibiscus plants seemed to greet them, "Bienvenidos" (welcome). If you wanted to be heard, you had to yell over the local cacophony. Micah drew even closer to Pops. At one point, Jackson thought he'd have to carry the child. Then he heard his name being called. He turned to the left to see Jorge trying to muscle his way through the crowd. He was shorter than he looked in his pictures.

Jackson held tightly to Micah and extended his other hand to Jorge. The Colombian clapped the older man on his arm. "Señor Jackson, eet is so good to see you." They hugged warmly. Jackson felt the love and sorrow emanate from this man. Those emotions matched the mixed-up array of colors in Jorge's shirt. The blues and grays overshadowed the lighter yellows and pinks.

He looked down at the child next to Jackson. Any shred of composure was lost when Micah, wide-eyed, spoke almost inaudibly, "Tío?" Jorge fell to his knees and allowed the child to fully embrace him as he scooped the boy onto his knee. Micah nestled his face into Jorge's chest. He repeated the word, "Tío, Tío." He could smell the woodsy smoke from the village on his shirt. He faintly recalled the aroma when he sat in the circle with his mommy and daddy. Micah drew in his breath deeply, drinking in the familiar scent of this man he called "uncle." Jorge choked out, "Yes, Micah, eet is your Uncle Jorge. I have missed you."

Micah tasted his own salty tears as he was rocked in the man's arms. "You have grown so much, little man. You look like your daddy."

He kept crying and clinging to Jorge. "My dad can't come to Cow-ombia anymore. Neither can my mommy."

Jorge burst into a flood of tears. "Yes, Micah, they cannot walk with us here on the earth, but they are in our hearts always. They are with you when you're in America and with me in Colombia. That is the beauty of how love can be in many places at the same time."

At this, Micah smiled. "Yes, Tío, Pops taught me we can still miss my mommy and daddy. But Jesus helps us when we miss them." Jorge could not speak. He just held the child and reached up to grab a hold of Jackson's hand.

When he clasped the hand, Jorge's mind set him tumbling back to the accident nearly one year ago. The rerun haunted Jorge with images of that dreadful day. Ugly memories stabbed his mind a thousand times, and now jabbed him again as he held this orphaned child.

His recollections deposited him back to three days prior to Rebecca and Tim's arrival last year. *They were going to bring new supplies. The villagers and I had looked forward to building another solid home for our neighbors. Women had cooked lots of local favorites and the delicious smells wafted in the air. I had sampled several dishes two days before I was scheduled to drive with the caravan to pick up the missionaries. There was an air of anticipation among all of us in the village to see our beloved Rebecca and Timothy. Micah's parents were revered by my whole community.*

The day came to retrieve the young couple from the airport. Last minute touches were being completed for the beautiful feast. Our reunion at the airport was sweet. After loving greetings, everyone pitched in to finish loading the three trucks. The irregular-shaped bundles were strapped down and hidden under blue tarps. Everything was secured and ready to roll.

Occupants bounced on old seat springs while traveling on the uneven mountain roads. The rainy season had left the roads wounded with holes. Winds had begun to whip at the vehicles and tossed one of the tarps off its truck like a kite. It got tangled in a set of trees on the switchback below. The trucks honked to signal each other to stop. When they all finally came to a grinding halt, I quickly jumped out of the truck and yelled over my shoulder to tell the others I would retrieve it from down the road. I remembered yelling, "I'll get it. I'll be right back." I jogged quickly to the grove of trees that wore the blue cover like a rain poncho. My arms ached as I wrestled to free it from the boughs. Just as I started to roll the canvas, the winds grabbed at it and fought me like a tug-o-war. The sky darkened quickly, and a fierce torrent of rain lashed wickedly at my back. I looked up to check on my friends on the roadway; what I saw terrified me.

It all happened so quickly. The jolt knocked me to the ground with a merciless thud. A thunderous noise and a surprisingly rich smell of earth accompanied the horrifying scene. Desperately scrambling to get my feet under me, I looked up to see a twisted deluge of trees, rocks, shrubs, and mud, so much mud, careening down towards the roadway where the three trucks were waiting. The trees snapped like toothpicks right before my eyes and the onslaught of mud picked up the trucks and the roadway itself. They were violently thrown like mere toys in the clutches of an evil monster. I could taste the blood in my mouth and choked on my own cry of sheer terror.

What once was the side of the mountain, was now a pulverized heap of smoking rubble. Dust, ash, and shredded trees lay in atrocious heaps. All were now buried beneath tons of mud and debris. The mountain had swallowed my friends, and everything in its path. Only I was left.

I never imagined I could recover from such a devastating loss. I buried myself in the tasks of village life as if to create my own suffocating tomb as a penance for not dying with the others. In the deep recesses of my mind I wondered if Emma and Jackson could ever forgive me for surviving when their own daughter and son-in-law had died.

* * * *

Micah was wiping tears from the brown weathered cheeks and asking, "Tío, you okay?"

This time Jorge buried his face against Micah's neck. His muffled voice was like a wounded animal, "Sorry, so sorry. Forgive me."

It was Jackson who now held Jorge and Micah together. "There is nothing to forgive, my friend. We can help each other heal, there's no blame here. The Lord will help us find our way through this difficult time."

Micah tugged at Jorge's shirt, "It's okay, Tío. Pops and me are with you."

The child's voice and Jackson's words comforted him. He thought, *Perhaps Señor Jackson is right. This is a time we can help each other heal from such a tragic loss.*

This was the first ray of hope Jorge felt since the accident even though jagged shards of dark memories remained in his heart. He turned Micah's words over in his mind, "We can still miss them, but Jesus will help us."

The Colombian glanced at the blue sky silently and uttered prayers of thanks for the flicker of hope kindled in his heart. Healing began as these three survivors held onto each other. Being together was like a blanket of comfort for each one of them. Everything **really was** going to be okay.

Breaking Through Pain

Jorge led them through the maze of traffic and people in the airport parking lot to the trucks, introduced them to the other men, and together they loaded luggage into the bed of the second vehicle. Ray, the two engineers, and Jorge reviewed the checklist to make sure all the equipment was accounted for. Micah announced his 'twitchy' belly felt better, and he wanted to sit up front between Jackson and his tío. Three of the men from the village jumped in the back of the green pick-up with the luggage. Ray blurted out, "Well, it looks like we're not in Kansas anymore. No strict road rules here." The two engineers chuckled when they joined their new Colombian friends for an open-air ride. This company was ready for their trek into the mountains.

Rutted roads slowed their progress but did not detract from the beauty of the countryside. Contours of lush green mountains appeared to be painted against a deep blue sky. Spidery clouds pointed downward to the valley below where water roared over large, gray river rocks. The trio of old weathered vehicles rounded the bend to see ribbons of water cascading down a lovely waterfall in the distance.

Against this scenic masterpiece was a mountainside dotted with tin huts. They reminded Luke of the strawberry farmer and his children in Mexico. He could still picture those two little kids with dirty T-shirts and their tiny pail. It prompted him to ask José, the driver, if the families here allowed their kids to work in the fields.

José answered, "Of course we do. But I think you North Americans might not feel the same when it comes to work and kids."

Luke shot back more defensively than he intended, "What do you mean by that?"

"We love our kids just like you do. To work alongside us in the hot mountains all day is too hard for the children. We give them tasks they can accomplish. Those tasks are difficult but the children take pride in being able to help."

Luke nodded his head in agreement, "Well, I can certainly understand that. José, if you don't mind my asking, where did you learn English?"

"My grandfather married a white missionary. She taught her kids and grandkids that we would need to speak English when more white men came to our country. She was right."

José continued, "Most of the people here have no desire to speak another language. They believe if you're in our country, you should know our language. Sound familiar?"

Luke grunted, "Yeah, we hear that in our country, too."

He spoke highly of his grandmother and how she told her children they were the sweet fruit of two cultures. She encouraged them to appreciate the traditions of both.

"Grandmother believed if you understood a person's culture, a love for the people would come naturally." José smiled remembering her often repeated phrase, "The gospel of Jesus is to love one another. That is how they will experience the Savior."

Luke enjoyed listening to this man and learning about him and his family. The travelers slipped into a comfortable silence as the trucks ambled along the road. Luke pointed towards tall, orange mounds of dirt and asked what they were.

"They're the homes of Colombian mountain ants. They have become an international delicacy. I'm afraid you won't get a chance to taste them on this trip because they're harvested in the spring." Luke was relieved it was the off-season. He was not in the mood to eat ants, even if they **were** a delicacy.

Suddenly, the caravan became shrouded in a fog like a dark tunnel. The far-off vistas disappeared. Sounds became muffled, and moisture began to lay heavily on the narrow roadway. The trucks began to downshift to compensate for the upward climb and diminished visibility. Only minutes before the fog enveloped them, Jorge had discreetly pointed out to Jackson the ruinous heap across the valley. He knew it was the place where Rebecca and Tim met their untimely plunge to death.

Jackson became acutely aware of the grinding gears, an acrid smell, and the sound of flapping tarps. He could feel the mist on the metal sill of the truck where he rested his arm. His stomach lurched, and he feared losing anything that remained of his lunch. Jorge sensed Jackson's misgivings. He leaned over and asked, "Are you okay, Señor?"

Pops bobbed his head mechanically. Silently. Jorge assured him the trucks would take a break once they were up and over this mountain. "Señor, it will probably take us fifteen minutes to get to a clearing where we can sit and rest outside the trucks."

Again, Jackson just gave a slight nod. Micah began to sing in hushed tones as he slipped his hand onto his pop's arm. Jackson did not respond to the soft touch. His only thoughts were of Rebecca and Tim. He wondered if the sound of a flapping tarp was the last sound they heard.

The physician was paralyzed, everything he touched felt hotter. His mind was singed with a repugnant, metallic odor. He desperately needed some air, even though the window was wide open.

There was a faint tinkling sound at the edge of his blackness. He clung to the life-saving cadence of the soothing sound. His hand slid against a wet metal surface as he clawed to rid himself of this nightmare. Desperate, he tried to focus on the sweet notes which seemed to call him away from his frightening drama. Jackson struggled to breathe. One more ragged gasp and he gagged and sputtered like an old engine.

Then the air suddenly changed. Lighter. Easier to inhale.

The trucks were at a halt now but Jackson was still frozen in his seat. Ray and Luke tugged at the door while Jorge caught the older man before he fell out. He was unable to hold himself up. The three men helped shuffle Jackson to a small patch of grass on the side of the road. José held the child's hand and remained close to Pops. One of the men ran back to the truck to get a canteen. The other men stepped back, not wanting to steal the air. Micah continued to sing, not quite sure if the song was to help Pops or to comfort his own pounding heart.

Jorge held the canvas jug up to Jackson's lips and encouraged him to sip slowly. Color crept back into his pale face. The emotional storm had begun to subside. Jackson looked up to see worry etched on the faces of the small assembly. Words still would not come until he spotted Micah who was singing slightly above a whisper. The child approached Pops and tenderly asked, "Do ya have pain in your belly or is it just twitchy?"

Jackson reached for his grandson and slid him onto his lap. They held each other and rocked as Micah's tune of 'Jesus Loves Me' faded into silence.

Pops looked at him, "Child, you saved me. Your song was like a faraway chime in a thick fog. It kept playing and I followed it. Thank you."

Pressing his mouth to Micah's ear he added, "We will always hold your mommy and daddy in our hearts."

He snuggled closer to his Pops.

Jorge croaked, "Señor, the Lord is busy mending our broken hearts."

"I was trying so hard to be brave, I actually forgot how necessary it was to grieve." Jackson tousled Micah's hair, "Like I told this young man, we can still miss them! His parents cannot be replaced but the Lord is giving us different people and experiences to enjoy in this life. It's amazing that Rebecca and Tim were the ones who paved the way for this new adventure to help others."

Pops looked up to see tear-stained faces of the men as they responded, "Amen."

* * * *

After the unsettling episode with Pops, Micah leaned against his grandfather and slept soundly for the rest of the trip. Jorge was relieved to hear Jackson's occasional snoring, too.

It was the cheers from the villagers as the trucks pulled into the grassy field that awakened the passengers. The travelers stretched and unfolded their weary bodies. Micah, wide-eyed, stayed glued to his grandfather's side. Jackson noticed the two engineers sticking close to their truck buddies while being introduced to the other villagers. Their bumpy travels in the back of the truck created a new level of camaraderie among those men. He marveled at the wondrous ways the Lord orchestrated meetings.

Ray, Luke, and Jackson were all greeted warmly but the special reception was reserved for Micah. Some of the younger children approached and handed him some sticks tied together. One of the ladies bent to greet Micah and handed him 'a cross'.

Micah tugged at Pop's arm and asked if he could run to the truck for a minute. He gave him the nod and a few minutes later Micah came running back to the circle with his backpack. He handed each child a stone. New friendships were being forged and old ones were being rekindled.

Lots of welcomes and even tears accompanied the reception. Jorge said it was time to take the tired Americans to their temporary home. They passed a large fire pit as they were escorted to a makeshift hut a short distance away. They later learned the pit was the community kitchen.

Jorge instructed them to place their personal belongings in the hut which was built from pieces of tree limbs, blue tarps, and ragged sheets of tin. Ray noticed large green leaves leaning against the corners of the crude building. When Luke bent down and pointed to the roughly hewn bowls below the leaves, they both realized they were looking at water collecting chutes. They shook their heads in admiration at the ingenuity of these people.

Inside the hut were grass mats beside each cot. Such a unique home base was an obvious outpouring of appreciation for the North Americans. Luke used his limited Spanish to express sincere thanks on behalf of all the men. When Micah ducked into their new home, he knew where he would sleep. Next to the smallest cot was a pouch with a few stones stacked on top of it. Micah smiled and relaxed. He turned to Jorge and asked in Spanish, "Who put these here?"

Jorge shrugged his shoulder. "A few of the boys remembered you enjoyed throwing stones with them. Maybe they were the ones who gave them to you."

Micah perked up, "I forgot that I like to throw stones. At home, I only collect them."

"Well, amigo, the women are planning a festive dinner tonight, maybe you'll find out who your secret admirers are when we all get together. The children are eager to see you again." Jorge tousled his hair and gave a laugh. He turned to the men, "I hope you're okay with the hut. Rest for now, we'll call you for dinner later."

The team stretched out on their cots and enjoyed a nap. The serenade by the late afternoon song birds signaled 'fiesta time'.

When they stepped out of the hut, the fire was roaring, and two large kettles hung close to the flames. The villagers were busy tending to the meal. The kids were off to the side not too far from their mothers' watchful eyes.

Two ladies and four children timidly drew near to Micah. They spoke deliberately to him in their native tongue and he replied in Spanish as if he never left Colombia. Jackson was utterly amazed. Even though the child spoke slowly, he had not forgotten the language. After some exchanges, Micah turned to his Pop and asked if he could go play.

Pops cautioned him not to wander too far. Micah and his friends ran to a small grassy clearing and began playing. The scene warmed Jackson's heart. It was as if his grandson was a part of their family. He could see why Rebecca loved these people.

Jorge and José assumed the roles of interpreters for the rest of the group. There was a lot of laughing and gesturing to get the gist of what was being said. It did not take long before they were fully engaged in getting to know one another.

After the greetings, everyone settled in for an authentic Colombian meal which consisted of rice, black beans, chicken, and arepas (ah-ráy-pahz) with goat cheese. The arepas are like Mexican tortillas and are a staple food here. The team filled their bellies with the delicious food. After the meal was done, everyone got a coconut adorned with a fresh flower and a plastic straw.

José laughed so hard when he saw the straws. The locals normally drink directly from the fruit. He explained to the visitors how Rebecca had generously supplied straws to the villagers. They wanted to impress the guests with their use of the modern-day tool.

Micah leaned over to Jackson and Luke as he said, "Remember drinking soda on the boat with Twizzler-straws?"

They all laughed as they enjoyed the coconut water. Micah slurped the coconut and swabbed the drippy remains from his chin, “Next time, we’ll bring the candy straws for our Cow-ombian friends.”

After the festivities everyone enjoyed viewing the myriad of stars, the woodsy campfire, and the crisp mountain air. Tomorrow would be a busy day laying out all the equipment. Jorge would show them the location of the previous well and the task would begin.

Micah's Dream

Unpacking and dragging the equipment to the dig site occupied the men for the next two days. Ray and the engineers ran soil tests and decided the location of the new well would be thirty feet west of the original one. A narrow footpath was the only access which created an additional challenge.

After three tiring days, all was quiet in the camp at the very early hour of four a.m. Jackson rolled over on his cot to see young Micah standing there rubbing the sleep from his eyes. "Hey, little man, are you okay?" Micah whispered and told his grandfather that he had a very important dream. Jackson unkinked his spine as he dropped his legs over the side of the cot. The child held his hand over the flashlight to avoid waking the others. "Can you give me a couple minutes to stretch, then I can listen to your dream?"

"Sure, Pops. I'll wait on your cot."

Jackson ducked out of the tent quietly. He arched his back gulping the rich, musky mountain air which began to wipe away the cobwebs of his sleepy mind. The stars were twinkling like millions of sequins in the sky. He breathed a prayer of thanks for the opportunity they had in this place. He asked the Lord to guide and comfort his sweet wife who was so far away. Upon returning to the tent he found Micah snoring on his cot. Jackson leaned toward him and the boy jumped up, "Pops, can we talk outside?" As Jackson followed Micah out of the tent, he reached to the right, ran his hand gently over the darkened mound, and grabbed one of the straw mats. Both Micah and Jackson tiptoed out into the humid night. Looking up with a reverent expression the boy leaned into Jackson and whispered, "Looks like we could touch 'em. Don't you think, Pops?" Jackson gazed upward.

The starlight illumined an eerie walkway between tufts of grass and low-lying shrubs. They walked gingerly a few more feet away from camp before they turned their flashlights to full beam. There was peace in these majestic mountains but they were in unfamiliar territory and remained close to camp. They found a good spot to open the straw mat and sit together. Jackson was lost in his own thoughts and Micah was thinking how he could tell Pops the dream just like he remembered it.

Jackson recalled the locals had given their beloved land the nickname of 'eternal spring'. Although the nickname referred to the year-round feel of spring weather, Jackson liked to believe the Lord was creating an opportunity here to tap into the eternal spring of the life of Christ. His heart cried out, *O Lord, Your Majesty is truly a sight to behold in the dark and beautiful mountains of Colombia.* He longed to have Emma by his side to enjoy this view, but the next best person in the whole world he would want to share this view with, was this little child sitting next to him.

Micah stood up as he began to speak in a hushed tone. He began to tell his dream, "Pops, the angel in the dream was very big. I never saw him in any of my other dreams. His skin is dark like the friends who live here. He's standing with a pipe in his hand. It looks like a handle to an old-fashioned water pump like the one we saw at Batsto Village. Do ya know which one I'm talking about?"

Jackson pictured the old pump in front of the little homes in the historic Batsto Village where visitors could learn about the Revolutionary War. "Yes, I know which one you're talking about."

Micah continued to recall the dream, "I could see rusty spots on the **big** metal pipe. The angel was holding a gigantic umbrella in his other hand." Jackson couldn't help but crack a smile at the picture being described. The young boy grinned, "I know. I laughed at the angel 'cause he looked so silly. He didn't laugh, but he wasn't mad at me for giggling at him. He moved the pipe up and down in the air like he was trying to get water. He was standing by a group-a-trees. It looked like the trees behind the village. He was pumping that pipe kinda hard. He stopped moving and tilted his head like he was listening, then he started pumping it up and down again in the air. Me and the angel laughed 'cause it looked so funny. We laughed so hard that my belly hurt. Then it happened."

"What happened, Micah?"

He began jumping up and down and holding his arms high above his head with his hands facing the sky, "It started to rain. My face was drenched and then my clothes were drippin' wet. My feet started to get covered with mud and then it rained so hard, that the rain washed my feet off. Then the water was up to my knees and it was running down the hill like a river. Then the angel said something."

Jackson urged him, "Go on."

Micah cocked his head as if hearing it for the first time. The angel said, "Our God **RAINS**." Then me and the angel laughed again and then I remembered what you taught me 'bout Kings **raining**. Remember when you taught me that kings **rain**?" Micah held his hands above his head and wiggled his fingers to demonstrate the drops.

Jackson could almost see the downpour.

The child went on, "I didn't get it. How could raindrops come out from a king? But ya told me it meant they are rulers on the earth. You said rain can mean two things. Water from the sky **and** ruling. Know what else, Pops?"

"No, Micah. There's more?"

"That angel smiled at me. A great **BIG** smile."

Jackson and Micah sat quietly for several minutes. The little guy got lost in his thoughts. Before Jackson had a chance to say anything, Micah spoke up, "Pops, we're NOT diggin' in the right place. The guys think we should be near the place where tío used to get water. But the angel's telling us to go behind the village near the tall trees?"

Jackson's tears streamed down his face. "You're an amazing little boy. Yes, I know the grove of trees you're talking about." They held hands and lay back on the woven mat together to look at the black sky peppered with its twinkling lights.

"What do ya think we should do, Pops?"

"Well, I think we should lay here and enjoy these few moments, then we'll go tell the others."

"Okay, Pops."

Jackson wiped the back of his hand across his tear-stained cheeks and squeezed his grandson's small hand. His thoughts crawled sluggishly into the scene at Batsto Village last year with Emma, Micah, Rebecca, and Tim. The five of them toured the historic village to learn about the War of Independence. The village residents had shared a common water pump. The Batsto well was not very deep, but it provided ample water supply for the entire community. Jackson could still picture little Micah trying to pull the pump handle up to see if he could get some water. Being so young, he didn't know the well had been dry for a long time. Tim was putting his face under the spout to pretend he was getting a drink. He never expected the soaking water to wash over his face and wet his shirt so thoroughly. As Micah muscled the handle, Rebecca stood behind her son and emptied her entire water bottle onto her husband. While Tim was sputtering and shaking off the water, the rest of us were doubled over in peals of laughter. Micah beamed at his accomplishment of getting a drink for his dad. It's hard to believe that was over a year ago. Jackson silently hoped the well they would dig here would be as productive for these folks as that old fashioned one was for the people of Batsto so long ago.

Streaks of orange and pink colored the heavens as the grandfather and child gathered the mat, brushed off stray grass, and walked back.

Just an hour ago, the celestial torches pierced their velvety backdrop. The world was sleeping when an angel gave a message to a child who had enough faith to listen and believe it was the voice of God. It was time to share the news with the others.

At the brilliant breaking of this day Jackson stood in the center of camp, extended his hands to heaven, and spoke in a strong, deep voice that resonated on the side of the mountain. The words echoed in the damp morning air, "This is the day which the Lord has made; Let us rejoice and be glad in it." The others stumbled out of their tents to see what was happening.

Jackson requested everyone to join him. After much commotion, the team gathered together to hear him tell them about the early morning encounter the youngest team member had. When it came time to tell the dream, Micah told it. Afterward, you could hear a pin drop; even the tree frogs withheld their croaking. Jorge broke the silence as he said, "What are we waiting for? It's time to get busy moving the tools. Will we need umbrellas, too?"

The two engineers from the Water Company were not quite as enthused as Jorge was to relocate their dig site. One of the engineers asked his co-worker, "Is he actually talking about moving all our equipment 'cause this little boy had a dream?" They both looked over to see their leader's reaction and waited for his instructions.

Ray felt in his heart, although it did not make any sense, this move could prove to be a modern-day miracle. The engineers were trained to read the data and trust their expensive equipment. The two of them stated emphatically that all data indicated the proper site to drill was where they unloaded everything the past two days. There was no indication that the other site was even viable. They wanted to trust Ray's call, but never had a **dream** been considered as the deciding factor for a dig site. He told the team he'd need a few minutes alone to consider this new information.

As Ray knelt on the rocky ground behind the hut, he could hear the whisperings of doubt from a few members of the team. It took some concentration to erase the foreboding thoughts threatening to choke out his resolve to hear the only reliable Voice. "Father, this certainly is a way to stretch my faith. I trust that You will continue to lead us and guide us in this venture. You've always helped me with my personal decisions, especially with the care of my Charlene and our children. Come to think of it, even when my decisions were not so good, You helped me unscramble things. I trust You. Thanks for Your guidance to help our new-found friends. Amen."

He emerged from behind the tent with some new directions for the day. The dig would be relocated to the exact spot the angel showed Micah in the dream. Ray explained to the men, "I believe the data we ran is accurate; however, it has been my experience if you have a gut check, or as I refer to it as The leading of the Holy Spirit, it's wise to listen!" The two engineers were not fully convinced they had a legitimate reason to relocate but they trusted this man.

The leader continued, "Men, I intend to take full responsibility for this decision. It will require some hard work to relocate everything since we have a limited amount of man power. If there are any additional days or money needed to complete the job, I will contribute the necessary funds personally. I do not want you men to incur any additional hardships to complete this task."

A slight commotion at the entrance to the village grabbed their attention. Jorge looked puzzled and said he'd find out what was happening.

Minutes later, Jorge and six other men came into the clearing where the early morning pow-wow convened. He signaled to Ray and introduced the men from the other village. "These men felt like they wanted to lend a hand." Two young teens came running into the circle exclaiming they wanted to help, too.

The other team members were staring in disbelief at the newcomers. Was this some kind of divine intervention? Jackson lifted his hands towards heaven and mouthed the words, "Praise be to the Lord."

A New Dig Site

New plans were thrown into action quickly. The Water Company men conducted an initial survey of the new site. Unfortunately, the trucks could only squeeze to the bottom of the hill. They would have to physically carry the equipment through rough vegetation to get up to the best spot for the well.

They returned to the initial dig site to inform the others of the dilemma. Ray explained the situation with the help of Jorge as his interpreter. The men from the villages assured him they did not consider the situation to be insurmountable. Trees and weeds were small obstacles if their reward would be a new source of water. The engineers dripped with admiration at their tenacity.

They wasted no time relocating the dig. Sweat glistened on strained muscles and brows during the undertaking. Women and children visited with pails of water and food to sustain the workers throughout the day.

As the gray curtain of evening began to steal some light, the men sat on a nearby log for a much-needed rest. Some tribesmen broke the quiet of the afternoon as they began to sing. A few of them got up and danced jubilantly as the others continued in song. Micah sang quietly along with the group. Luke leaned down and asked what the words meant. The child looked up, "They're singing, 'Our God Reigns'."

When Jackson overheard Micah, he joined the chorus in English. The whole group erupted in a soulful worship song in both languages. It was a melody that echoed in the mountains hidden in the heart of this beautiful country. When the song ended, a sacred hush rested on all present. It reminded Jackson of the first meeting at Luke's house when they prayed for the favor of God. He sensed a strong presence of the King Who Rains!

Ray stood and said, "Let's get back to camp before it gets dark. Today we tapped a beautiful well of enthusiasm.

Luke added, "Hopefully, we can tap an even deeper well, mañana (tomorrow)!"

Drilling

Ray and the engineers formed the 'trio' who determined the location of the well. The three of them along with two of the other team members fought their way through thick foliage to stand on the spot where they would drill. Machetes were swung expertly to level the ground for the battery-operated motor. When they finished, they broadened the path back to the trucks through the dense trees. With the slightly wider trail, all the men lined up like an old fashioned 'bucket brigade' and heaved pipes, the motor, and tools from the trucks to the dig site. Three of the locals remained near Ray and stacked the pipes that would soon be burrowed into the ground. After the materials were all in place, the men made their way back to convene at the bottom of the hill. The two areas were now designated as the 'upper site' and 'base camp'.

The men at the base were maneuvering sieves onto five-gallon buckets in preparation for them to be filled. A couple hours had passed, and Luke was about to holler up to Ray to ask about the progress, when the roar of the motor split the serenity of the countryside. Surprise and satisfaction etched the faces of all. Shortly after the engine had christened the air, the trio made their way down to the trucks. Ray announced, "We're all set for a great start tomorrow. It looks like AX-S is gonna like her new home."

* * * *

The next day Ray kept four extra men at the upper site to help maneuver equipment. They handled eight-foot lengths of pipe which housed the flexible cannula. Ray and the men wrestled the pipes down the shaft after the drill pierced through rock and dirt inch by agonizing inch.

It was a tough morning. As the group gathered for a midday breather, wispy clouds cast dancing shadows on the earth shading the men from the intensity of the sun. The entire team was positioned in an intimate circle surrounding the spot they all hoped would provide water. They were discussing the harrowing event from earlier in the day when the drill bit got hung up and could not penetrate through rough terrain at nine feet below. The tension was palpable. They drew in their breath hoping the bit would not snap. Like an unseen set of teeth chomping inside the earth, the drill cut and moaned trying to break through the compacted area. Worry crept in and hung low on all the men. The bit needed to be changed twice which was not a good sign. They feared this would mark the end of the road for this project. Time dragged on and the sound of the drill finally announced its success. A collective sigh of relief was expelled by those at the base when they heard the bit make its way through.

During the break Luke remarked, "That was nerve-wracking at the nine-foot mark."

Ray agreed, "At the base, you could only hear what was going on but those two partners of mine did a great job. They worked that motor like the experts they really are. They understood how to push it and when to lay off. Drilling does not fall into the category of simple."

He responded, "Hopefully the results will be worth the effort."

Sitting back at the village after the demanding day, one of the engineers was drawing in the sand with a stick. Jackson asked him what the picture was. He described it to the entire group and a lively discussion ensued. The drawing was a schematic of a good solution of how to transport the water from the well down to the trucks. Before it was time to get some sleep, most of the details were ironed out. They'd find out tomorrow if the plan could be implemented after they re-examined the site.

Day Five: Trying New Plans

At the dawn of day five, everyone awoke energized, eager to set up the troughs that were designed in a dirt sketch the previous night. Upon arriving at the site, only Ray and one engineer resumed positions at the drill while the third expert led the others in the construction of chutes to transport water to the base. They rigged ropes and aluminum gutters to build makeshift spill-ways. The tangle of trees was hard to work through but proved to be excellent braces for the water slides.

After a challenging morning working in the middle of roots, vines, and a plethora of spider webs, the group climbed from base camp to join the engineers next to AX-S. Heads looked up to see Ray stepping through some underbrush at the edge of the site. He approached his co-workers and clapped them on the back, "I'm thrilled to have these men with us. They were the ones who had the fortitude to include aluminum gutters on our supply list. Team, great job on that chute! Looks like you guys got a good start."

The next three days Ray assigned different jobs for the men to accomplish. Rotating the tasks kept morale high. At the end of day seven as they gathered by the trucks, he announced, "While the rest of you were fighting ropes and wild Colombia to complete the water chutes, we were able to drop through to twenty-one feet today." Despite tired bodies, a great cheer arose.

Micah piped up, "When will we get water?"

Ray smiled, "You just keep helping the team get ready and before you know it, we'll be swimming in it."

* * * *

Everyone was busy whether they were clearing more brush, securing lines on the gutters, or running final lengths of hose to the back of the trucks. Every day they loaded buckets onto the beds of the vehicles in anticipation of hitting water. So far, they had to unload those pails every night without water.

They had grown accustomed to the drone of the engine. When loud cheers dropped down the hill from the upper site, the base camp froze. This time Jackson hollered, "Ray, what's happening?"

"We did it. The slightest moisture just spurted up the cann."

"Can we join you up there?"

"Absolutely. We'll hold off 'til you all get up here."

The entire lower camp made a mad dash to clamor to the upper site. When they managed to fight through the tight pass to stand together as a unit, the drill began again. They witnessed water burp itself out of the top of the tube in slow motion. It sputtered and coughed up some grainy, tea-colored liquid.

Jorge and José both wiped tears from their brown faces.

The trio worked quickly to attach a spigot to the top of the protruding tube. They poured the water into specimen cups to run some tests. Their audience waited silently until one of the engineers exclaimed, "Good river. This is exactly the kind of results we'd hoped for."

The mountains had not experienced this type of celebration in a long time. The ground vibrated under dancing feet. Jackson had a strange sense the river of water deep below was sloshing in response. He shouted above the noise, "Ray, how far did we drill to hit it?

Flashing ten fingers four times. Jackson stared in utter amazement. Forty!

The engineers indicated they'd need space to perform the next three strategic moves. Men pressed themselves close to the outskirts of the work area to give them room. All eyes were on Ray and his colleagues.

Their revered leader held up a small pouch of pellets. He told the team the best they could hope for would be a puff of gray smoke rather than black. If it was black, they would have to re-ignite the pellet sack. Hushed, the team observed the pouch and detonator as they were released down the chute.

A hollow thud accompanied the brief discharge of gray smoke. Some of the team members gripped each other's hands firmly as if willing each step to proceed without a hitch.

The third engineer slid the prepared ball of fabric down the cann, following it with a blunt-tipped probe to make sure it wedged itself at the bottom.

The company watched his expression and knew the results were not good. He looked up at the crestfallen faces and said, "Let's increase the size of the netting."

He repeated the process with a slightly larger ball. Again, he inserted the probe and exclaimed, "I can feel the material, it must have been able to plug the opening this time."

Next, Ray pulled a face mask over his mouth and nose, then snapped the latex gloves on his hands, "Jackson, does this bring back memories of practicing medicine?"

He answered, "Keep your head on the project. Don't get distracted. Those chemicals can set you reeling."

Micah said, "You kinda look like an alien."

He smiled at the boy and got busy pouring the syrupy solution into the tubing. The chemicals were toxic and emitted an unpleasant odor. It would take roughly five minutes to glue the mesh ball to the walls of the cann. As the group waited, they fell into whispers among themselves, so they wouldn't disturb Ray. The gentle breeze in the mountains stirred the leaves in the nearby trees. Luke noticed some ants trekking across the dusty earth and wondered if these could be the edible ones. Almost in response to his silent musings, he looked up to find José grinning and shaking his head no. He quietly said, "No, Luke, you'll have to return later to enjoy the world-famous delicacies." Luke responded with a bright smile.

After Ray was finished, the engineers expelled air down the cann to expand the fabric into the stream. One of the men shouted above the din of the motor to let everyone know the netting was in place and they were ready to draw water for some new tests.

The results from the next samples tested much cleaner. The tightly woven fabric was doing its job in the river below. He explained, "Looks like we'll only have to add a few drops of purifiers." All eyes turned to the cann when it began to quake furiously. Ray and his men had to grapple with the hose and spigot as it wriggled out of their hands. It snaked its way on the ground and spat water like a fire hydrant. The men were diving out of the way of the wild rodeo hose. Luke dove on it as if he was taming a bucking bronco. Ray ran over and grabbed the nozzle to try to cap it. Two more men jumped on the hose to wrestle it. Finally, Ray threw his hands up in victory when he got it capped.

The dazed men looked around at the filthy scene. Dripping wet with sludge, some men stood ankle deep in puddles while others sat sprawled atop a mound of soggy soil. All were dumbstruck. Mud had exploded onto all the equipment and every member of the team. They all stood thoroughly baptized in it.

Micah laughed uproariously and shouted, "The angel was right. Our God **Rains**!"

The next explosion was of men running amok with shouts of jubilation. Mud-covered bodies embraced one another. Jackson yelled, "It looks like we hit the proverbial jackpot… of water!"

The men reveled watching the three young boys continuing to slosh in the murky puddles. Micah's wide grin and sparkling hazel eyes stood out in contrast to his muddied body.

Ray and Luke bellowed in unison, "Yee-haww!"

Hugs. Dancing. Jumping. Hollering. Their achievement was monumental!

Good News for the Villagers

Elation spilled over in both villages when the mud-spattered men returned late in the day. The people dripped with appreciation as they hugged the well-diggers irrespective of their muddy garb. Afterwards, Jorge gathered the troops and led in a solemn prayer of thanksgiving to God for sending them such a wonderful team of people and the treasure of fresh water.

Later, as they sat by the campfires, Jorge asked Micah to stand. The children approached him with a gift. One of the young friends acted as the spokesperson and thanked the six-year-old for listening to the angel in his dream. Everyone applauded when he held up the cherished gift. A sling shot.

Micah sat himself once again between Jorge and Jackson. The grandfather proudly hugged him, and Jorge leaned over to promise the little one he would make plans to visit him in the United States. Micah responded, "Tío, I think Lita needs to see you and hug you like I did. It might make her cry, but tha's okay."

Jackson and Jorge exchanged smiles.

The festivities continued until the twinkling of the starry sky replaced the light of the torches.

* * * *

The next day water careened down the chutes suspended in the whispering trees to the base of the hill. Men directed nozzles to allow a manageable flow into the buckets. Each vehicle transported the precious liquid to the waiting villages. Women and children hoisted the smaller vessels to be emptied into the new fifty-gallon drums. It was a beautiful communal effort that occupied everyone for hours.

Throughout the day, the 'trio' organized the upper site to make it as user friendly as possible. Jorge and José would be the newly dubbed water engineers who would operate the well when the rest of the team returned to the States.

Tired bodies shuffled to sit by the evening campfire at the end of the day. After some tearful good-byes and promises of returns, each one drifted into their huts to fall asleep one last time in these mountains. The visitors had learned of this land which held luscious water reserves deep in its belly and riches of incredibly loving and simple people. The hut echoed with whispered discussions of flowing water and the possibility of ongoing friendships.

Flying Home

The group felt pampered as they sat on cushioned seats in the air-conditioned plane after ten eventful days in the mountains. A steady, low hum inside the aircraft lulled most of the team into peaceful sleep. Jackson looked over at the child napping next to him and noticed his occasional smile as the sling shot rose and fell rhythmically on his small chest. The man wondered if he was encountering another angel in his dreams.

Pops started to hum the tune of "Our God Reigns" before he joined the others in a land of sweet dreams.

Stateside

Annie and Luke

On the couch Annie snuggled closer to Luke and was glad for the unseasonal chilly air. They watched the embers flicker up the chimney. The glowing red and occasional burst of orange created a light show infused with a delicious woodsy aroma.

Luke draped his hand gently on Annie's growing belly. His eyes widened as he felt their child stir. Annie lit up, "Wow, did you feel that?"

"Yeah. Is that the first time you felt it?"

"Yep. She waited till you got home."

"How cool. Does it hurt?"

"No, it feels like butterfly kisses."

"Oh, like when you bat your eyelashes against a kid's cheek?"

"Yeah, it's so slight. I'm so happy we felt it together."

"Me, too."

Annie shifted her body on the sofa, "I'm relieved to have you home and I'm happy things went well in Colombia. Do you think you'll go back again?"

Staring into the fire with a faraway look, "Yes. I'll go back. There was one particular time when I thought about you more than any other time."

"Really?"

"It was either day four or maybe five. Anyhow, the drill got stuck. It grinded and basically refused to go further. We could smell the gears down the hill. It was scary. We were not sure if it would halt the whole project." He looked at his wife and stroked her cheek lightly.

"When it stalled, I thought of you and your struggles just a few weeks ago."

She bent to pick up her glass and waited.

He continued, "It took you some time to figure out that fear of having kids was causing a major roadblock in your life. But the whole time you were dealing with those issues, I felt out of place, almost useless."

She groaned.

"Early on, when I was with the team, I didn't feel very helpful. Kind of like a tag-along. Then one of the days when I stood in line with the other guys, handing pipes to the engineers, I realized my part."

Her smile urged him on.

"I was part of the support team in Colombia." He turned his full face toward Annie, "While you were plowing through a bedrock of obstacles to get past fears. I was your support."

Annie grew solemn, "I'm sorry you felt so helpless. I guess I was trying to get through my struggles. Grabbing a piece of jade along the way helped me cut through those fears."

"It was worth the wait. It was great when you finally broke through. It was amazing in Colombia when we were able to drop deep into a crystal reservoir of water far under the ground."

"Hey Hon, here's another strange correlation. You guys hit water at forty feet." Annie rested her hand lovingly on her belly, "And after forty weeks of pregnancy, we get to hold our prize."

He grew thoughtful, "I never made that kind of connection. This conversation is way deeper than I thought. No pun intended. So, before we get too deep, can you finish filling me in on what happened around here while I was gone? This time I want details."

"Well, let's see. Last night I told you about the crazy excitement with Charlene, Scott, and Emma when I broke the news. It was like an explosion. So much fun. I was on cloud nine for days, then to top it all off, Charlie and I went to one of Emma's prayer meetings. We thoroughly enjoyed it; those ladies are something else."

"Are they all pretty old?"

"Most of them are older but there are a few younger ladies too. They welcomed my sister and me like we were part of their little group."

"If they're anything like Emma, they're good people."

"True. We spent some time chatting about our families. After that, they got right down to the business of prayer. It was so natural. No stuffy feeling. Do ya know what I mean?"

"I think so. Like, very personal?"

"Exactly. When they pray it's not like they're begging, it's like they're stating the facts about something. I can't explain it clearly."

He asked, "Did it feel like the time Jackson prayed here during our first meeting about Colombia?"

"Yes, like that! **And** Emma spoke about the prophetic word she received months ago."

Luke sat up taller.

"A lady from the prayer group had told Emma to prepare herself for a separation which would result in a great accomplishment." She continued excitedly, "That night at our home, when Jackson mentioned he wanted to take Micah on the trip, Emma had remembered her friend's words. That's what gave Emma peace about the guys leaving. She told us prophetic words are like God giving you a clue about something in your life now or something coming into your life. They can give you encouragement or strong direction. The Lord sometimes uses words or pictures that hold special meaning for the person receiving it, kind of like a secret message between them and God."

"When we were on the trip, Jackson explained it almost the same way. The word can be as basic as a Bible verse, but it hits with a powerful impact because it's exactly what the person needs to hear."

"As you were saying that, I remembered when the jade got returned to Emma and Jackson, they spoke so kindly to me. It was like getting a shot of confidence. **Those** were prophetic words for me!"

The young parents-to-be sat in their own bank of swirling clouds until Luke resumed, "My question is, how did we miss learning about this stuff? I mean we've been Christians for a long time and it's important to speak prophetic words; they can actually help people. How come we didn't learn this earlier?"

"I thought about that too. Maybe we weren't ready to learn about prophecy. We wouldn't teach a kindergartener how to fix a car engine. We probably needed to grow up to be ready to accept these things."

"I don't think it's so much about growing up. Micah had a dream about an angel and he knew it was important. He actually had an interpretation. Really, dude, you're only six!"

Annie giggled, and Luke went on, "Maybe it's because he's heard prophetic words, dreams, and angels since he was a baby. He views those things as a perfectly natural way God talks to people. But, Annie, we didn't think those were ways God would speak to us, did we?"

She exhaled loudly.

"Look how unusual we thought your dream was about riding a bike and wearing a green sweater. We made fun of the fact that Charlene would have a chance to practice interpreting a dream. Well, maybe I shouldn't say **we**, maybe it was just me being ignorant."

She said, "Nah, it was definitely both of us."

"It's almost like we didn't believe God would talk to us in a dream. We wake up from a dream saying it felt so real, but we don't take the time to find out if there was a message from God. And prophetic words, we scoff. Silly! We ignore them and walk past, not listening."

She asked quietly, "And now?"

"Now?" He stared at the coffee table as if trying to read a new script. "How can I turn back to what I used to believe after the experiences of the past few months? Things are different."

"Do you mean, now we look for the direction of God in **any** way He wants to communicate with us?"

Moments slipped by before Annie resumed, "Do you think the stone that Jacob slept on caused him to have his dream?"

"Are you talking about **Jacob** in the Old Testament?"

After she shrugged, he laughed lightly, "I'm not sure if it's the pregnancy, but you are all **over** the map with some of the things you come up with."

"Sweetheart, you have NO idea the places this mind has explored these past few weeks."

He touched her knee. "Go ahead. This new train of thought sounds… umm, interesting."

She sat up on her heels, "Okay. Remember the story in Genesis 28 when Jacob was traveling to Haran, he stopped to rest in Bethel." She reached into the drawer, grabbed the Bible, and flipped it open. "Listen to verses eleven and twelve… 'And he came to a certain place and spent the night there, because the sun had set; and he took one of the stones of the place and put it under his head, and lay down in that place. And he had a dream, and behold, a ladder was set on the earth with its top reaching to heaven; and behold, the angels of God were ascending and descending on it.' In the dream God was letting Jacob know about his inheritance."

Annie opened the drawer again and fished out some papers. She leafed through them as she started, "In some parts of the Chinese culture, jade is considered to be very precious. They believe the stone has significant spiritual properties. Some claim it to be the Stone of Heaven. In the Chinese language jade is called 'yu' which means heavenly or imperial."

"Cool. I've heard of imperial jade."

She flipped to another page and said, "Other ancient cultures called it **The Dream Stone**. Some of those people believed there was a connection between the calming properties of jade and the dreams people had. Even today jade is thought to promote insightful dreams. When I read that, it made me wonder." Annie looked deeply into Luke's eyes.

"So. Do you think it's possible that Jacob's pillow was jade?"

He furrowed his brow.

She sucked in her breath, "The green gem has been discovered in the country of Jordan, which is right next door to the land where Jacob had his ladder and angel dream."

He leaned slightly forward.

She went on, "My dream with me riding my bike was right after I found the stone. I didn't put it under my pillow or anything like that. But that dream set me on a journey. Do you think God used the jade I found to help me?"

The Livingstons sat quietly until Luke broke the silence, "Pheww. That's a lot of ideas swirling in that pretty head. Honestly, after being directed to the exact location of where to dig a well by a six-year-old dreamer, I'm not crossing **anything** off the list of how God speaks or what He uses to get our attention. In answer to your first question, I do believe the stone Jacob slept on could have been jade. Those folks had a deep connection to the earth and believed their environment held naturally healthy elements."

"When did you become an expert in ancient civilizations?"

"I'm not an expert but I **have** read a lot of National Geographic."

Annie broke into a brilliant smile.

"I have one caution to add to all this."

"Sure."

"Jacob **might** have slept on a stone of jade, but it doesn't mean all dreamers will have that experience. Look at Micah. I don't think he slept on a rock; yet, look at his dream."

"I totally agree. God used a stick to part the Red Sea, but it doesn't mean all sticks will separate a sea. I get it."

"Hon, I think the big lesson here is that we can't limit how or what God will use to speak to us. Even if it seems unlikely, we can't dismiss it too quickly."

The mother-to-be looked down at her belly and said, "I think we're learning all this in the nick of time. When this little one arrives, we can teach her about the deep things of God early in life. Then she won't think any of it is strange or unusual. She'll learn early to listen to prophetic words and recognize angels in dreams."

"We'll have to pay close attention when she tells us about her dreams. God might use our child to direct us."

"Oh, Luke, this is so exciting."

"Sweetheart, ever since our Mexico trip… No, I have to correct myself, ever since you found the stone, life has been different for us."

"Absolutely. The stone, the Rhineharts, fishing trips, Mexico, and Colombia. Yikes, that's a lot of different."

He tapped her belly and gave her a penetrating look, "And the most important one!" They sat back in each other's arms.

Annie whispered, "We've learned so much lately. As for tonight, it's just you and me and the baby."

"Glad I went on the trip and I'm even happier to be home. I love you, Annie Livingston." He leaned down to Annie's middle, "And you too, Baby Livingston."

Ray and Charlene

Ray was stunned no one had spilled the beans about the baby until yesterday afternoon when the team planted their feet back on American soil. He was remembering the conversation with his brother-in-law when he told him the good news about his Annie. Ray had said, "I wouldn't have allowed you to come on our Colombian adventure if I knew your wife was pregnant."

"That's why we decided to wait to tell everyone. The real miracle was that Annie kept quiet until we left. As soon as we stepped foot on the plane she exploded the news to your wife and Emma. Then the girls had to keep the secret from you guys until we returned home."

"That has to be the best kept secret in this family!" Ray looked hard at Luke and said, "Hey, this explains a few things. Did you know about the baby when we were at the park and you had apples for Andrew and Micah?"

With a sparkle in his eyes he replied, "Yep. It took a lot of self-control not to respond to your comment about me eventually being a good dad."

Ray clapped Luke on the back and shook his shoulder. "What a great way to end our Colombian trip. Congratulations, Brother!"

After the conversation with Luke last night, Ray slept like a log. When he awoke in the morning, he entered the kitchen to find Charlene with her face close to her cup inhaling the aroma of the Colombian coffee. She breathed out, "Ahh. That smell.

There's no coffee like Colombian." She closed her eyes and let the aroma wash over her then she poured another mug for Ray. She balanced herself on the contoured crutch, handed her husband the steaming mug, and continued, "Sweetheart, when I learned Annie was pregnant, I cried for two days. It made so much sense why she was so moody and emotional lately. Remember when she served us water at their house when we were first discussing Colombia and she burst into tears?"

"Wait! She knew she was pregnant then? Wow, I'm **impressed** she waited all that time to tell you."

"She did good. My little sister having a baby, I'm thrilled. I can't tell you how much baby-talk we enjoyed. It was a fun trio of girl time when you guys were gone. Emma enjoyed us as much as we enjoyed her. She's been helping Annie with some cooking tips too."

Ray smiled and refrained from any comment about her learning to cook. He gave Charlene a mischievous smile before she swatted his arm playfully. He said, "Okay, looks like we're gonna need time for you to tell about your adventures while I was away. How 'bout if we go to The Bay Restaurant for a nice lunch?"

"Really, just the two of us?"

Ray put his hand over Charlene's, "No matter how far I travel, **you** are my world, sweetheart."

She beamed, "I can be ready in an hour. What about Andrew?"

"Handled! Liz is going to take him to the park to meet up with her friends. She said she doesn't mind at all."

"Then it's a date. I'm so excited."

The Rhineharts

Jackson and Micah were raking leaves as Emma busied herself on the back porch. She was humming and sweeping around the old, wicker furniture. It crossed her mind that this furniture was going to need more than a bright yellow gingham tablecloth and some fancy white doilies to brighten it. She made a mental note to ask Jackson if he could spruce it up with a fresh coat of white paint next spring. After she swept the whole porch, she went inside to prepare some home-made crab cakes and salad. She added walnuts for some crunch.

Emma saw the boys trade rakes for rides on the rope swing. Micah was laughing and chanting, "Higher, Pops, higher." A small flutter squeezed her chest as she placed the lunch tray on the table. She plopped onto the chair and gently massaged her ribs between the two top buttons of her blouse. At first, she thought it was the excitement of having her boys home from Colombia, but the tightness felt more like a burning lately. She vowed mentally to pay closer attention. Emma looked up as her men headed to the porch. Jackson instructed Micah, "Go wash up for lunch."

"Okay, Pops, bet I can beat ya to the bathroom." He started to run into the house. Emma refrained from correcting him. She wanted to enjoy his childish antics; besides, she noticed Jackson stepping up his stride trying to beat Micah to the sink first. She let out a laugh and began humming yet another song as she finished setting the table for lunch.

When the guys joined Emma, she said a beautiful blessing for the meal. The doctor simply closed with, "Amen." They each dug into the delicious spread of food and enjoyed cherished time together after a long, ten-day separation.

Susan and Emma

Emma was glad Susan had time for a visit after the prayer meeting. She swung the porch door open with a welcome, "Thanks for stopping by. Would you like to stay for lunch?"

"I thought you'd never ask."

The hostess served up two beautiful blue and white porcelain bowls filled with home-made pea soup. Susan admired the historic, farm pattern. Two crystal glasses of iced tea lay on the table decorated with fresh sprigs of mint and thin slivers of lemon. She told Emma, "You can make the simplest food look and taste like an elegant meal." The girls split a large grilled cheese sandwich topped with slices of tomato and avocado, served on thick multi-grain bread from the local baker.

"I serve my family and friends as the treasures they are to me."

"True, and I've seen you serve perfect strangers with the same fervor."

The two friends enjoyed the leisurely lunch. Afterwards, the guest queried, "So, my friend, what's on your mind?"

"Well, lots of things. I'm feeling nostalgic or appreciative or just plain ol' emotional lately. Anyhow, the past few months have been so full of changes."

Emma walked over to the fireplace mantle and brought down a golden picture frame with a photo of Jackson and Micah holding up the first flounder the child ever caught. She looked lovingly at the picture as she described that eventful day. "That boy was bursting with excitement when he handed me the fish. I was beyond happy to see his little face so lit up. It brought tears to my eyes to look up and see my Jackson beaming with pride."

She quieted as she shook her head to untangle herself from those sweet recollections. She blew her nose and wiped away a few happy tears.

"You have every right to be nostalgic and emotional. As a matter of fact, I think it would do you good to talk and sort out the things on your mind."

"That's only the beginning? I feel like I need to unclutter my whole brain. Do you mind listening?"

"God only knows you've listened to hundreds of hours of my life! It's your turn."

"Thanks, can I get you some coffee; this might take a while?"

She held out her cup, then fluffed the pillow behind her back. It had an embroidered design of a tropical bird with orange and red plumes. She was sure it was another gift from their Colombian friends.

When each cup was filled with hot coffee, she began, "I think I'll start with Micah. You were so right when you said it would be better to treat him like the grandmother that I am, rather than trying to treat him like Rebecca would. I still coax him into handling his youthful responsibilities, but we are much more relaxed with each other. Do you know he even says 'Lita' with enthusiasm again? Jackson made a comment about Micah's easy interaction with me lately. How precious!

Then there's Annie. I'm almost ashamed to say she feels like a daughter to me. I want to cry to think that anyone could ever replace my Rebecca." She choked out, "I had no idea this would be so difficult."

"Seems to me Annie might be filling some wound in your heart, but she will never fill exactly the spot Rebecca occupies. Your girl will always hold the biggest part of your heart."

"It's true, absolutely no one could ever replace my daughter. Annie **is** filling some deep needs in my broken heart. It's as if she is helping me and in some strange way I seem to be helping her too. She makes me laugh, especially when we're cooking together. It's funny how she never acquired those skills from her sister. Which brings me to one of my newest friends, Charlene. She's an amazing woman, sister, wife, and mother. She carries a grace about her despite so many physical struggles, she walks as if she's walking on air. I think it's her attitude. I'm eager for you to meet her. Then there's Ray and Luke. Two interesting young men. According to Jackson, they worked tirelessly in Colombia digging the well. He felt it was truly God's leading that brought the team together. Both of those young men are gems."

Susan stood up to stretch her back. Standing at the window, she began to strum her fingers on the sill. She glanced at the old, wooden desk that stood to the right. The quill pen laid on the hollowed-out space for pencils. She imagined Emma sitting there in the evening, dancing that quill upon the ivory sheets of paper, spilling out beautiful life tales. The Rhineharts were dear friends who lived life to the fullest. Their experiences could fill a book.

After listening to the clock's steady cadence, she asked, "What's really happening with all these ponderings of yours? It feels like you're holding something back. Am I right?"

Emma stood abruptly, "We're not getting any younger you know!" It came out stronger than she intended.

"OK. And why are you telling me what I already know?"

Emma pulled the desk chair out and plopped herself down. She uncapped the little bottle containing the rich black ink and began scribbling curlicues and feathery strokes absently. Susan waited patiently for her friend to recapture her fleeting thoughts.

"Jackson and I have discussed this idea for a few weeks. We don't have any close relatives. We each have some distant cousins, but they are even older than we are. Micah is only six years old. Even though he's an easy child, we don't know if we'll have the energy to raise a teenager or if we'll even be alive then. We have considered asking Annie and Luke to be his legal guardians should anything happen to us."

Her friend looked around for the other chair and pulled it across the corner of the gray and gold carpet. Sitting close, she placed a hand on her knee. "You're an amazing woman, Emma Rhinehart. God has blessed you with lots of wisdom. Remember when Annie first found herself on your sidewalk? Jackson told Luke the Lord orchestrated meetings for His own good purposes."

The memory shone in Emma's eyes. Her friend continued, "Besides the great adventures you have already enjoyed with the Livingstons, I believe **THIS**, right here, what you're speaking about now, is one of the main reasons the Lord brought you together."

Emma cried, "But I almost feel like I'm giving Micah away."

Susan gave her shoulder a little shake, "Nonsense! You are looking out for him. You would not have gotten up the courage to mention this to me if you did not sense the importance of this decision."

"I guess you're right."

"Of course, I'm right. And in case you haven't noticed. The Lord has been extremely gracious to you and Jackson, especially during these past few months."

"How so?"

"He has allowed you to feel comfortable with the Livingstons and their extended family. If something ever happened to you and Jackson, Micah would be very well cared for. He would have no trouble blending into their family. That child will never forget you or Jackson. The Lord will provide for all his needs. Our God has never failed us and He's not about to start now."

Emma broke down completely. She allowed the floodgates of grief and concern to wash over her. Hair hung in loose tendrils around her face and was moistened by the free flow of tears. Her long-time friend held her gently as she shuddered and quaked with each new wave of emotion. After Emma regained some of her composure, Susan went into the kitchen and prepared a cup of tea for each of them. When she returned to the living room, Emma was fast asleep among a mound of bright pillows on the sofa. Her friend draped the rose-colored blanket on her.

Susan took her tea and retreated to the kitchen. She held a finger to her lips when Pops and Micah came in the back door. The look that was exchanged between her and Jackson told him that she knew about the idea of guardianship. She smiled gently, approvingly. Jackson's shoulders dropped, and he exhaled deeply.

Micah piped up, "Hi Miss Susan, where's Lita?"

"She's taking a nap in the living room."

He ran upstairs and grabbed Mr. Cuddles. Stepping quietly into the room, he placed the fluffy bear in the crook of his grandmother's arm.

Susan turned to leave and gave Jackson a strong squeeze on the arm. She said quietly, "We serve a mighty God. He's in the details of our lives."

Jackson bent down and embraced this woman, their friend.

Micah came over to join them.

"Thanks, Micah, there's something special about a hug."

The Question

Three nights later, Jackson welcomed Annie and Luke into the house. "Thanks for coming. Emma will be here in a couple minutes. She took Micah over to visit Henry and Susan to feed the fish in their backyard pond."

The young woman said, "We are curious as to what this meeting is about, Jackson."

He responded, "I hear Emma coming in the back door now. Shall we sit in the living room?"

Luke glanced at Annie and gave a little shrug.

Emma came in saying, "Perfect timing. Do either of you want a cup of coffee or pie?

Luke answered for both, "No thanks. We're wondering if everything's okay?"

Jackson brushed by Emma and she appreciated feeling his warm touch on her arm. "We don't think this is an urgent matter, but it is important to me and my wife."

The younger man unconsciously leaned slightly forward on the edge of his seat. He said, "We're all ears."

"We have carefully thought about this matter. We think it's wise to have a plan in place to care for Micah, should we not be able to do so at some point in time."

Emma chimed in, "If anything happens to us, we want to make sure Micah's in good hands." Glancing at Jackson, his nod of approval fortified her to continue, "So, we want to ask you two if you would consider being Micah's legal guardians? If the need arose, we feel that you would care for him like he was your own."

Luke and Annie both sat dumbfounded. They were each adjusting to the idea of being parents in March. What was being asked of them could possibly make them parents sooner if anything happened to this precious couple. She instinctively put a hand on her belly. Luke scooted over towards his wife and balanced himself on the side of her chair.

Jackson looked at them, "We're not expecting you to answer us at this moment. We are asking you to think about it. Praying about this type of thing is certainly wise."

Annie held Luke's hand and his eyes. He answered, "Jackson, Emma, thank you for thinking so highly of Annie and me to ask us."

"It's almost as if we're already family. I don't like the idea of anything happening to either of you. I feel like you're adopting us by asking us to be guardians."

"Would you mind if I took my wife out back for a few minutes. I'd like to speak with her privately."

The Rhineharts stood up and offered to go into the kitchen, but Luke insisted that a stroll out back would be better for the younger couple. Pops nodded, "Of course."

Luke and Annie stepped outside to the sound of a breeze playing with some of the newly fallen leaves. She snugged her green sweater around her shoulders. He clasped Annie's hand in his as they strolled on the carefully placed stepping stones. The gray slate created a beautiful pathway next to the shrubs on the outside edge of the property. He commented on the stones and how they made the path so easy to follow.

She brightened, "Do you realize how many times the Lord has used stones in our lives to direct us, especially lately?"

He smiled, "Maybe He does that because of our name. Did you know that my original family name was Livingstone, ending with an 'e'?"

She scrunched her eyebrows together, "You never told me that before."

"I don't think I ever had a reason to tell you. It really does feel like stones play such an important part of our lives."

"Besides stones, there was another idea that crossed my mind. It might sound farfetched."

"Uh-oh. Does it involve traveling to a foreign country?"

She pushed his arm saying, "No. Not this time."

He looked at his wife quizzically.

She replied to his glance, "Do you think after I found the stone, the Lord had to knock me off my high horse, or bike in my case?"

"Do you mean an attitude problem?"

"Yeah. With this kind of decision in front of us, it would be important for me not to have a selfish attitude. I don't want to be like Saul in the Bible when he had to get knocked off his horse?"

"Whoa, slow down. I'm not trying to derail this new train of thought, but I want to set the record straight. Saul did **not** fall off a horse."

"Yes, he did. Remember in the book of Acts?"

"We can look at it later. But I can tell you there's no mention of a horse."

Annie shook her head. "Well then, I guess comparing my outlook to Saul's is a moot point."

"I disagree. I can see the similarities in your stories. Saul had his deeply imbedded ideas about who God was. It took a flash of light, him falling to the ground, and a voice from Heaven to adjust his mindset. Your eyes were opened when you found a green stone, fell off a bike, met the Rhineharts, sent me to Colombia,...

She interrupted, "Okay, okay. I get it. When you put it like that, I do see how Saul's story is like mine. Ultimately, we both saw the light."

They stood together under the canopy of a star-lit sky. Their individual thoughts broke into different recollections which helped them to focus on the main reason why they were here at this very moment.

The young woman's mind flipped like a stack of cards. The first card was Micah's little face as he offered her a very bouncy ball. The next was his sad outburst when he confessed to taking a stone from Colombia. Lastly, the picture of Micah blowing her a kiss with Mr. Cuddles.

Luke had his own separate memories. The look on Micah's face when he caught his first fish on the boat. How they practiced the art of burping. The gradual softening in his Annie towards kids when she watched us two boys catching fireflies in this back yard. Then he fast-forwarded to the team in Colombia and the tribesmen singing in Spanish. Micah's small voice telling Luke with a far-off look in his eyes, "The song is, 'Our God Reigns'." What an amazing little guy.

Luke pulled his wife gently to himself and looked into her crystal blue eyes. "Annie, it feels like I'm already a dad to Micah."

Burying her head in his chest, she responded, "We could not have orchestrated **any** of this. I believe it's a story penned from heaven."

They knew for certain what they would discuss with Emma and Jackson.

He whispered, "Are you ready to walk back and talk to the Rhineharts?"

* * * *

The four of them continued to enjoy another piece of apple pie and some coffee. Emma said, "We did feel like the Lord put you in our lives for lots of reasons, but this is the most important one. We're not planning on leaving this earth anytime soon; however, we need to be prepared for any unexpected events."

Jackson agreed, "Rebecca and Tim would have loved you guys. Micah is crazy about both of you. He already thinks of you as family."

Annie announced, "Micah is one special boy. To take on a closer role in his life would be an honor. You guys will always be Lita and Pop. This step is only a formality."

Jackson said, "Yes, but an important one."

Emma added, "Annie, we believed you and Luke would say yes, but we did **not** want to pressure you in any way. Jackson and I have a little gift for you, we hope you like it."

The older woman emptied the contents of the blue velvet pouch into a cut-glass dish. It chimed like a bridal salute on the edge of a champagne flute. She held the dish out to Jackson and he turned to ask the young woman, "May I do the honors of placing this around your neck?"

Luke observed the magnificent polished green gem in a stunning white-gold setting. Annie looked at the delicate piece through teary eyes. Jackson rose and clasped the necklace around her as if adorning a queen.

Emma bent and hugged her.

Tearfully, Annie ran her fingers across the jade dangling elegantly against her smooth skin. She stood up and embraced Jackson, "You've become like a father to me."

Tears glistened on the gray stubble of his cheeks as he held her, "Annie, you have filled a deep wound in my heart. Bless you, daughter."

Epilogue

Nine months later

Jade had just gone down for her morning nap. Luke loved looking at her rosy little cheeks peek out from under that soft, pink blanket. He wondered if she was dreaming when she uttered those little coos and occasional snores as she slept.

Annie and Micah were riding bikes around the big block. Micah said, “These trees are like giant umbrellas. We could even ride here in the rain.”

“I think you’re right. When I take Jade for a walk, I’ll make sure to tell her about the umbrella trees.” Annie ducked to miss the low branches.

“Can we stop at the bridge to look at the water?”

“Sure.”

Pink and white dogwood petals drifted happily on the stream. Undisturbed until the six-year-old dropped a pebble and separated them. They rocked on tiny ripples and were scattered.

Micah stared at the petals shifting like a collage jostling for their rightful positions. Pointing to a particular cluster, he gasped, “Hey, look! My stone pushed them together.”

He aimed the next nugget to see if he could separate them, but the stone missed its intended bullseye. Instead a new sprinkle of color emerged as foliage and flowers snuggled. Curling together. Tighter.

Annie quipped, “Looks like your stone shoved them closer to one another. Did you know God uses stones to teach us important things?”

Fingering dirt off the next stone he absently asked, "Huh? You mean stones can talk?"

"Not exactly. But they do have a job." She slid the jade back and forth on the chain around her neck. "Here. Remember this one?"

"Yeah."

"Well, God used it to introduce you and me. We're kinda like the petals bumping into each other because of it."

"Oh, cool. That stone bumped me, Lita, and Pops into you, Luke, and Jade."

"Exactly."

Pointing towards the water he quipped, "Well, I like how pretty those petals look down there."

"Me, too."

The child set another stone free. The splash set Annie back three months ago. They were standing in the kitchen when Emma had dropped her crystal water pitcher. Pieces of what used to be were changed in an instant. That afternoon Luke picked Micah up from school. It had to become the new routine until his grandmother was released from the hospital. An eerie hush had settled in both households for those few weeks. It was ironic when Annie became the cook for the Rhineharts during Emma's recovery. The elder woman was so proud of her student's progress.

Baby Jade softened Micah's adjustments of staying with the Livingstons during that time. Every day, Annie or Luke took Micah to visit his grandparents in the afternoons. It helped to comfort his heart and gave Jackson the time he needed to tend to Emma. Each time Micah returned to the Livingston's he would spend time making Jade laugh when he told her all about Lita and Pops.

When the time came for Micah to live with his grandparents again, Luke commented on how easily the boy adapted. He learned to be as comfortable with the Livingstons as with his own grandparents. Luke and Annie would later appreciate the trial run of having Micah live with them.

Annie hesitated, “Micah, can I ask you a question?”

“Sure.”

“When we first met, you told me I’d probably be going in an ambulance if it wasn’t for my angel. What did you mean when you said that?”

He looked at Annie as he remembered, “Oh yeah. When you fell off your bike I saw the angel with you. She didn’t catch you, but she moved some rocks out of the way. I’m glad you didn’t hit your head on them.”

“I didn’t even notice any rocks.”

“Yep. The ball bounced on them.”

“Oh, so what did the angel look like? I don’t think I’ve ever seen an angel.”

“Well, she looks like a little girl.”

“Really?”

“Yep. She wears a hat.”

“What kind of hat?”

He stared a few seconds as if he was picturing the angel, “It’s a cute little girl hat. It’s pink with some fancy white stuff on it.”

She stared at him. “Lace? Is it white lace?”

“Yep. That’s it.”

She mused, *my favorite childhood hat.*

When he finished tossing stones, they got started on their bikes again. Annie thought of this beautiful young dreamer who sees angels and has become such a part of their family.

She never would have imagined these two families would flow together so perfectly. Annie proudly wore the very stone that God used to bump this irregular group into a newly formed family. Who would have dared to dream it?

She beamed knowing her beautiful daughter Jade was now one of the precious gems among the living stones that God fitted together so brilliantly.

Acknowledgments

My sincere thank you to:

My husband Joe who believed in me long before I put pen to paper.

Karen Oliver, who did not scare me away even after she handed me my first bloody manuscript. Thanks for your red pen ministry and your expertise of the English language. Any flaws herein are my own, not Karen's.

My son Matthew for spending many hours reading aloud and making great suggestions. Thanks for letting me grieve over my character Charlene when I discovered she had Multiple Sclerosis.

My son Patrick and his keen eye for details. Your enthusiasm energized me to complete the project when I began to have my doubts.

My son Jeffrey for our long phone conversations. Thanks for your coaching words, "You've got this, Mom!"

Catherine Daly for explaining in medical detail and visual demonstration how an IV works.

My mom-Lupe Bernicker, brother Bill McManus, and my sisters Veronica Breunig and Diana Hatton. Thanks for always being in my corner offering love and support.

Joe and Karen Stabler and all those faithful people who attended the prayer meetings. I still read the prophetic words. They continue to light my path.

Karen Longo, Linda Ryan, Sharon Schmidt, Laurie Angerman, and Leslie Glickstein. Each of you are special friends and I appreciate your texts, cards, walks on the boardwalk, time in the 'glory' pool, 'coffee' breaks, and prayers throughout the writing process.

The Writers' Group of Linwood Library: Jacki Kellum, Dorie Lord, Philip Mappin, Lanee Phillips, Jane Zhiying Hu, and Lynn Miller. A talented group that knows how to bring the best out in each other.

Anne Giordano for your creativity. You offered your help at the perfect time.

*May '**The Dream Stone'** bring glory to God who sees me and all of you as precious gems.*

52155973R00116

Made in the USA
Middletown, DE
08 July 2019